MW00577210

THE
WILD MUSTANG
& THE
DANCING FAIRY

USA TODAY BESTSELLING AUTHOR
SAFFRON A. KENT

Copyright

Cover Art by Najla Qamber Designs

Editing by Olivia Kalb and Leanne Rabesa
Proofreading by Virginia Tesi Carey

April 2021 Edition
Print ISBN: 9798512369357

Published in the United States of America

Chapter 1

Two years ago…

Bardstown High

He has beautiful gray eyes, gunmetal gray that sometimes glow in the night.

So much so that people call them wolf eyes.

His jaw is sharp and angled, a true V, and his skin looks like priceless marble. Again, so much so that people say he's got wintry, vampire skin.

They say he's got magic, dark magic, running through his veins.

If a girl so much as looks into his pretty wolf eyes, no one can save her from falling for him.

No one can save her from getting her heart broken either.

Because *he* never falls. He is mighty. Everyone knows that.

He's a heartbreaker. A player.

People say he doesn't even have a heart, or if he does, it's pitch black.

But he knows how to toy with yours.

He knows how to play with it. How to toss it up in the air just for fun and how to tie it up with strings and play with it like a puppet. And when he gets bored, he knows how to let it slip through his fingers and drop on the ground, breaking it into tiny little pieces.

Yet girls can't help but come back for more. Over and over and over again.

They can't help but come back to the Wild Mustang.

Or the Mustang for short.

That's what people call him. That's his soccer nickname.

He plays soccer, yeah.

Soccer is quite popular in our town. In fact, he's the soccer legend of Bardstown High. And he's as majestic and magical as an untamed mustang. As reckless and edgy and completely mesmerizing.

Although I don't call him that.

The name that *I* get to call him is something completely different, something that I've come up with after a lot of deliberation and thought: a villain.

That's what I call him.

A Gorgeous Villain, actually. Because well, he is gorgeous, but he's a villain, and I have good reason to believe that.

Four good reasons.

Four overprotective, overbearing, *older* reasons. My brothers. Who hate him with all the fire in their hearts.

Well, not all of them hate him with *all* the fire in their hearts. Only one of my brothers does, Ledger. The other three just hate him a normal amount.

Why does Ledger hate him the most though?

Because the Gorgeous Villain is Ledger's soccer rival.

My brother plays soccer too and he's a legend in himself. They call him the Angry Thorn, because my brother is a hothead and our last name is Thorne.

Anyway, they both play for the same team. And should potentially be friends and have the same agenda.

However, they aren't–friends, I mean. And they *don't* have the same agenda, at all.

Probably because they're both forwards for Bardstown High. One is left wing and the other is right and basically, they're supposed to help each other.

But they don't because they have this ongoing, age-old contest, where whoever scores the most goals in the season wins.

It's a matter of pride and honor and a whole lot of testosterone.

I don't know how it got started, this contest, rivalry, whatever you want to call it, but they both take it very seriously. Their whole team, which is divided into my brother's camp, the Thorn camp, and *his* camp, the Mustang camp, takes it seriously as well.

So does the whole town.

Whoever wins this unofficial contest becomes the reigning champion. This year it's my brother – he won by one measly goal last season – who also happens to be the captain of the team.

The whole town treats him like a king.

Which means free drinks, free food at local restaurants, posters on park benches and light poles. Back pats from people on the street and of course, all the attention from girls.

Trust me when I say that these two will go to any lengths to be the winner.

They'll do anything to mess with each other, ruin each other's game on and off the field just so they have a better chance of scoring goals.

And for years I've heard about it, about their rivalry, about *him*.

I've heard how corrupt he is, how evil and twisted. How he'd do anything to win at soccer. How much of an asshole, douchebag, bastard, motherfucker, and all those things he is.

But of course, I can't call him that. I can't call him all those names.

I'm a good girl.

I don't curse.

Besides, my brothers curse enough for all of us.

Hence the name: A Gorgeous Villain.

Anyway, it's game day and I'm at the soccer field right now.

A little personal confession: I don't like soccer. Not at all.

I think it's boring and I'd rather be home right now, either baking cookies or cupcakes, or knitting in my favorite arm-chair by the fire. Two of my favorite things to do.

Another personal confession: I don't understand this rivalry either. I don't understand this whole need to win and be the best at any cost. I mean, they play for the same team, don't they? If the team wins, they win, correct?

But as I said, I'm a good girl and so a good sister.

I'll always support my brothers. No matter what.

They're my whole wide world. I love them to pieces, and I know they love me to pieces too.

So here I am, sitting on the bleachers, watching a game I don't really care for, just so I can support Ledger and cheer for him.

And also Conrad, my oldest brother, who happens to be the coach of our high school soccer team.

So soccer is not only this town's sport, it's also our family sport; my other two brothers, who are away at college right now, played for Bardstown High as well.

This kind of makes me soccer royalty by extension.

But anyway, good. That's what I am. A good girl. A good sister.

Good. Good. Good.

Are you, Callie? Are you?

Are you really a good sister? Are you really cheering for your brother, Ledger, or are you also cheering for him?

Oh my God.

Blasphemy.

I'm not cheering for *him*. I would never ever cheer for

him.

He's the enemy.

Yes, he is.

He is. He is. He *is*.

My agitated thoughts come to a halt when someone – a frazzled-looking girl – stumbles and almost falls on me. My arms automatically shoot up and clutch her shoulders to help keep her balance.

Even though I manage to save her from falling, the tub of popcorn in her arms tips and a flurry of kernels falls on my lap and my feet.

"Oh my God, I'm so sorry. Are you okay?" she asks as she manages to straighten up.

"I'm fine," I assure her, brushing popcorn off my dress. "Are *you* okay though?"

"Yeah. No," she replies, and clutching the huge tub of popcorn to her chest, she raises her finger in a gesture for me to wait. Looking back, she shouts at someone, "Asshole." Then she sighs and plops down on the empty seat beside me. "Ugh. I hate this. He wouldn't move his leg. Idiot." She rolls her eyes before fixing her gaze on the field. "And I was so excited for the game tonight. Am I late? I'm late, aren't I?"

"Maybe a little." I shrug. "But nothing's happened yet. It's 0-0. It's the day of the defenders. So, you're good."

She smiles. "Thanks." Then she thrusts the tub of popcorn toward me. "Want some? I already spilled on you, so."

"Sure, yeah. Thanks." I pluck out a few and pop them in my mouth. "I'm Callie, by the way."

"I'm Tempest. Nice to meet you." Her smile is bright and friendly. "So I'm assuming you go to school here?"

"Yup." I nod. "And I'm assuming you don't?"

There's something familiar about her. I can't put my finger on exactly what though. But I'm pretty sure I haven't seen her before.

She shakes her head at my question. "Nope, I'm just crashing the party. I go to school in New York."

"New York? That's exciting."

"Meh. I completely hate it there. I miss home too much." She shrugs. "But anyway, I wanted to be here for the game. I'm supporting someone. He's gonna completely freak when he sees me. He has no idea that I'm here. You? Are you supporting someone too?"

"Oh yeah. I'm…"

My words get swallowed up when she bends to set down the container of popcorn.

Because I understand who she's talking about. Who's going to completely freak when he sees her.

It's written in the back of the t-shirt, or rather soccer jersey – in school colors, green and white – that she has on. The name and the number.

In bold black letters, Jackson, 11.

She's here for him.

The Gorgeous Villain, my brother's rival.

Reed Jackson.

Actually, Reed *Roman* Jackson.

That's his full name. And all us freshmen call him by his

full name.

Well, except for me. I already call him something else, but yeah.

To freshmen, he's a celebrity. A shiny star to admire from a distance. An awe-worthy creature.

And she's here for him.

"You're here for R-Reed?" I blurt out instead of answering her question.

I not only blurt it out, but I stumble on his name too.

Like it's a roadblock in the dark. A jagged rock on an otherwise smooth trail in the woods.

Something that trips you. Makes you fall.

Something that you don't see coming, not until you've already fallen.

"Yeah." Tempest gives me a quizzical look. "Why?"

Avoiding her eyes, I clear my throat, feeling embarrassed. It doesn't matter that she's here for him. Lots of girls are here for him.

He's a playboy, remember?

"Nothing. I just noticed, uh, his name on your t-shirt."

"Do you know him?"

"Not at all," I say quickly. A little too quickly and it only increases her suspicion. So I immediately follow it with, "I-I mean, except for the fact that he plays for the team. My brother plays too."

That seems to distract her. "Your brother?"

Okay, good.

I don't want to talk about him. I don't even know why

I got so jarred at the fact that this girl, Tempest, has specifically come down from New York to visit him.

It's none of my business.

"Yes," I say proudly. "Actually, my other brother is the coach."

"Other brother?"

"Yes. I have four."

"Holy shit. I can't handle one."

I chuckle. "I know, right? Brothers can be…"

"A pain in the ass with all their protective shit?"

"Yes." My chuckle turns into a laugh. "Exactly. They can be a little overprotective."

"A little? My brother is the very definition of overprotective. He is *insane*." She rolls her eyes. "If he had his way, he'd lock me up somewhere and wouldn't let me out until I was thirty or something. A thirty-year-old virgin. Imagine that."

She fake shudders, making me laugh. "Your brother sounds like my brothers."

Which is the truth.

My brothers are overprotective and it can be annoying sometimes.

But I don't begrudge them that. I don't begrudge them their overprotectiveness and all their rules and curfews, their genuine worry about me.

Mostly because we don't have parents.

Our father took off just after I was born and our mother died of cancer when I was four.

So they've brought me up, you see.

Together, they've taken care of me, loved me and protected me more as my parent figures than my brothers.

Especially Conrad.

"But I guess they do it out of love," I continue, "since we're all we've got. I don't have parents, so we take care of each other."

That makes Tempest smile. A sad sort of smile but a smile nonetheless as she says, "Me too." Then, "Well, I do have parents but they're as good as nonexistent so my brother takes care of me and I *try* to take care of him."

I smile then too.

I've never met anyone who has understood this, understood what it feels like to have no parents and only siblings.

But I guess this new girl gets it.

What a fun coincidence.

"So your brother," I chirp, wanting to know more about her. "Does he go to school in New York too?"

Oh and does he know Reed as well?

How do you know Reed?

Why are you here for him? Do you like him? Are you...

God.

I need to stop.

It's none of my business.

She isn't the first girl to be in love with him and she won't be the last. If anything, I should probably warn her about him.

I should tell her that he's never ever going to reciprocate her feelings.

Because all he does is break hearts and makes girls cry.

"Nope. He goes to school here. He's a senior," Tempest replies.

"Oh! Who is he?" I ask. "Maybe my brother knows him. He's a senior too."

Before Tempest can answer though, there's a roar around us and we both get distracted. The crowd is cheering and the reason for it is apparent as soon as my eyes land on the field.

It's him.

He's the reason, the Wild Mustang.

He has the ball in his possession and he's not giving it up. The players from the opposite team are chasing him. They're almost crowding him in from all directions, all their defenders against one Reed Roman Jackson.

And for a second it looks like they might be successful.

They might take the ball away from him.

The whole stadium is expecting it. All the people who are watching, they expect Reed to lose the ball. It's in the way that they've all gone silent and the way the announcers are talking with a rapid-fire speed and a louder tone.

But they're all wrong. Every single one of them.

Like the way they're wrong about the fact that Reed is a mere athlete.

He's more than that.

He's not only an athlete, he's also a dancer.

Look at his footwork. It's exquisite. It's impeccable. It's graceful. It's the envy of every dancer, especially a ballet dancer. And I'd know because I'm a ballerina. Have been since I was five.

Reed Roman Jackson has the kind of footwork that

would make any ballerina fall in love with him.

It would make any ballerina go down on her knees and weep at his feet.

Not me though.

I can't.

What kind of a sister would I be if I did?

Therefore, I can't widen my eyes at the rapid swipes and the swings of his legs as he zigzags through the closing-in crowd, still somehow keeping possession of the ball. I can't wring my hands in my lap when he nearly crashes into a guy from the opposite team. I can't lose my breath when he almost loses the ball but at the last minute, with a fake pass to throw them off his scent, he saves it.

And neither can I hop up from my seat and clap and scream when he finally, *finally*, sends the ball flying with such force that it feels like it's slicing the air itself in two before hitting the net and scoring the goal. The first goal of the game.

I can't do any of that.

I can't.

But I can't deny the rush in my chest or the puff of re-lieved air that escapes through my parted lips.

I can't deny that my veins feel full and bursting.

They feel full of music, of the notes of a violin, and my feet are restless. So restless to just… dance.

"*That's* my brother."

Tempest's voice pierces through and I jerk my eyes away from Reed, who's getting thumped on the back by the Mustang camp of the team while the Thorn camp is simply going about their business of getting back into their positions, including number twenty-three, Ledger.

"Um, sorry. Who's your brother again?" I ask because I completely missed who she was pointing at.

She throws me a sly smile. "The one you've been watching."

"What?"

She bumps her shoulder with mine. "The one who scored the goal just now and you got so excited that I thought your eyes would pop out of your head."

"I didn't."

Did I?

She laughs. "You so totally did. Even I don't get as excited as you did."

My heart is a drumbeat in my chest. "I –"

"It's fine. I won't tell." She mimics a zipping motion on her lips before pointing to the back of her jersey. "But anyway, Jackson. I'm Tempest Jackson. Reed's my brother."

She's Reed's sister.

Sister.

"That's why you look familiar," I breathe out before I get a hold of myself. "I'm sorry. I just thought you looked familiar."

She wiggles her eyebrows. "You also thought I was his girlfriend, didn't you?"

"What? No." I shake my head, squirming in my seat. "I… It's none of my business."

"It's okay. He has a lot of girlfriends. Oops. Not girlfriends. Girls. My brother doesn't do girlfriends."

"Oh yeah, I know."

Tempest stares at me for a few seconds. It's not long but it's enough to make me slightly uncomfortable and self-conscious. "But that doesn't mean that he won't ever have a girlfriend. You know, when the right girl comes along. He's just being an idiot right now."

"O-kay." I nod. "That's good to know."

"Is it?"

"What?"

Tempest completely turns to me then. "I like you. I think you're cool. And I think…" She lowers her voice. "You have a major crush on my brother. And –"

"Oh my God. Stop."

I look around to make sure no one's listening in on our conversation.

Although the stadium is so loud and people are so engrossed in the game, I highly doubt anyone could eavesdrop even if they wanted to.

But still.

I can't take any chances. If someone so much as got a whiff of the fact that I was talking about him, that Ledger and Conrad's sister was talking about having a crush on the enemy, I don't even know what would happen.

Ledger would definitely kill Reed. *Definitely.*

And then he'd lock me up somewhere for who knows how long for betraying him, and I wouldn't even blame him.

Because it is a betrayal, isn't it?

"What?" Tempest asks confused.

"Don't even talk about it."

"Why not?"

"Because you can't. And because *I* can't."

"You can't what?"

I look around again. I even go so far as to lean in toward her and lower my voice. "I can't like your brother."

She leans in as well. "What? Why can't you?"

"Because I can't."

"Yeah, you said that. But what does that mean?"

"It means that I can't. I'm not..." I look for a suitable word. "*Allowed.*"

"You're not allowed?"

"Nope."

"Well, who is it that's not allowing you?"

I stare at her a beat before saying, "Look, you don't live here so you don't know."

"What don't I know?"

"There's bad blood between my brother and yours." She frowns and I explain, "My brother hates your brother and the feeling is mutual, okay? So don't even talk about these things."

Her confusion has only grown. "What? Why?"

I go to explain the whole thing to her but turns out I don't have to.

When I can show her.

Because what happens at every game is already happening on the field. The two star players of Bardstown High are facing off against each other.

You'd think that ever since Ledger became the captain, he

would try to steer clear of all kinds of fights and arguments. At least on the field. But no.

Because Reed doesn't let him.

Ever since Ledger became the captain, Reed's aggressiveness on the field has only grown.

I'm not sure what brought on the current argument but they're standing toe to toe.

I can't see their expressions from here so all I have to go on is their body language and it is not looking good.

There are tense shoulders, rigid backs. Wide, battle-ready stances and folded arms.

I can read my brother like a book and I know he's angry. I know that the vein on his temple must be pulsing as he says something, or rather, snaps it at Reed.

Who, on the other hand, appears completely relaxed.

Reed looks like he doesn't care that Ledger is almost up in his face. He doesn't care that Ledger looks like he might hit Reed at any point.

But I think it's all for show.

It's all to provoke Ledger, to show him that he can't get to Reed, to mess with his head.

Reed's successful too because in the next second, Ledger shoots his hand out and pushes Reed back.

Oh God.

And finally, we have a reaction.

It pulses through Reed like a current, obliterating his relaxed persona, making him rigid and unforgiving. And when Reed takes a threatening step closer to Ledger, Ledger does the same, bringing them back to standing toe to toe, their bodies sweaty, their heads bent toward each other as if they're exchanging confidences rather than threats.

The two beasts, the Mustang and the Thorn.

Just when I think that they're going to start punching each other, someone steps in.

My oldest brother and their coach, Conrad.

He absolutely hates this rivalry. *Hates*. He hates Ledger's anger. He hates Reed's recklessness.

He hates the fact that every high school team in the entire freaking state knows about this. About how the two star players of Bardstown High can't quit measuring their dicks on the field — his words, not mine — and they always take advantage of it.

My oldest brother gets between his two players, plants one palm on each of their chests and pushes them away.

When he's managed to break the two heavily panting, angry-looking guys apart, Conrad wraps his large hands around the backs of their necks and pulls them in again, giving them a piece of his mind.

When he's done Conrad straightens up and pins them with his hard gaze for a few seconds before letting them go. And just like that the game resumes.

"So that's *my* brother," I tell her, repeating her words. "The one who was clearly trying to beat your brother up. Ledger. And the one who got between them? The coach? That's my brother too, Conrad."

"Oh wow," Tempest breathes out.

"Yeah." I nod. "See? You can't even joke about it. Not in

Bardstown."

She keeps staring at the field for a few seconds before turning to me. "So... I don't think you're gonna like what I'm going to say next."

"What?"

"That I think *I* have a huge crush on *your* brother." Her gray eyes — so unmistakably like Reed's — pop wide. "I've never seen someone stand up to my brother like that. Ledger."

She breathes out his name in a dreamy voice.

"I don't —"

"Oh, and you're coming with me," she speaks over me.

"Coming with you where?"

"To the party."

"What party?"

"The aftergame party that Reed always throws."

Chapter 2

I'm going to a party.

But that's not important.

That's not even on the list of top three important things.

It's not as if I haven't been to parties before. I have. A few times.

But between school and my dance classes, I don't get a lot of free time so I'm not that experienced with them either.

The ones that I have been to were loud and overcrowded and had really bad music.

Not to mention, they sort of freak my brothers out.

They don't show it though, no. For my sake, my four overprotective older brothers try to hide their worry.

They try to hide the fact that every time I go to a party, they're all always watching the clock. They're always watching the door too – well, Con does because he likes to stay home, the rest of them are usually out and about with their friends – and texting each other to see if I'm back.

I think they have a group chat together.

I mean, we have one where all five siblings are included but I think they have a secret four-person chat where they sort of obsess over if I'm okay.

I guess even though I'm in high school now, I'm still their baby sister.

The one who followed them around while growing up. The one whose ballet recitals they all went to. The one who couldn't fall asleep by herself for the longest time when our mom died, so all my brothers would take turns during the night and stay with me in my room.

I don't really remember that part, about not falling asleep by myself, probably because I was only four when Mom died, but every time I think of it, I can't stop crying and smiling.

I can't stop the rush of love I feel for my big brothers.

So over time I decided not to go to parties at all.

I don't want to worry them for something I don't really have the time for and don't like to begin with anyway.

But I'm going to this one.

And I'm going without telling my brothers.

That's their *one* rule – to keep them updated about my whereabouts.

They'll let me go to parties, or to the movies with my friends, but they need to know where I am at all times.

They don't know where I am right now.

They *think* they know; I texted them saying I'm studying with one of my friends and that I'll be back by my curfew.

They don't know that I'm here.

That I'm going to a party thrown by Reed Roman Jackson.

My brother's rival.

The guy I'm supposed to stay away from.

And I have.

I *have* stayed away from him.

I have been extremely careful never to be in the same place as him.

If he's in the courtyard with his friends, I'm in the library. If he's in the cafeteria, sitting in his usual spot, I know to stay on the opposite side of the room.

If I see him sitting inside his Mustang in the parking lot after practice, listening to music with his eyes closed, I turn around and walk through the soccer field to get to the bus stop.

Basically, I have done everything in my power to stay away from him.

So I don't really know what I'm doing here.

I don't even know how it happened. How I got pulled into going. By his sister, no less. Who I met only a little while ago.

But one minute we were watching the game and I was explaining to her about the rivalry, which I'm so glad to say that she doesn't really understand either. And the next, the game is over and Tempest is pulling me away from the field, telling me that we shouldn't be controlled by our brothers' stupidity.

That I should ignore all the rivalry stuff and go to a party with a friend — *her* — if I want to. And besides, if I don't like it,

I'm free to leave.

So here I am.

Going to a party with a friend who has promised me that I can leave if I want to.

And I want to, I think.

Because as soon as I see the crowd, I realize that this is even stupider and more dangerous than I originally thought.

This party, which is happening in the middle of the woods that border Bardstown, is full of people from the Mustang camp.

The soccer players who worship him, the students from Bardstown High who are in awe of him and girls from all over town who want to be with him.

All of them are either laughing or talking or swaying with the music with red cups in their hands. I even hear people chanting his name off to the side.

Of course, Callie. This is his party.

This is his territory.

Everything here is his.

Except me.

I'm the trespasser. I'm the one who doesn't belong. I'm the anomaly here.

And what if someone recognizes me, the sister of his rival?

What if they tell Ledger about it?

Oh Jesus Christ, I haven't thought this through, have I?

I have *not* thought this through at all.

What if he uses this, me being here, as something to rile Ledger up in the next game?

He's done it before.

I mean, he hasn't used *me* to rile my brother up. But he *has* used things against Ledger. And well, Ledger has done the same, but yeah.

I need to get out.

I need to leave.

I grab Tempest's hand and try to stop her from getting into the thick of the crowd. "I think I'm…"

Going to leave.

That's what I was going to say before I left my words hanging.

Because just then the crowd parts, the horde of swaying bodies falls apart, and there opens a direct line of vision.

To him.

The guy who owns everything around me.

Reed Roman Jackson.

He's sitting on a log, his powerful thighs spread, his demeanor casual, his body leaning forward with his elbows resting on his knees.

And as usual, he's not alone.

There's a girl draped over him — I think she's from school — and she's talking to him, whispering something in his ear.

It's not the fact that a girl is hanging off his arm that makes me pause, no. I've seen this before at school, multiple times. I mean, it would be more of a shock to see him *without* a girl.

It's not the girl. It's him.

It's the fact that despite very meager lighting in the space

— the moon and headlights from parked cars — every single thing about him is so clear, so vivid.

So *alive*.

Like his hair, for example.

His spiky, dark hair. The strands of which have little droplets sitting on the tips, making me think that he just had a shower, right after the game.

And maybe he was in a rush to get to his party.

Because he didn't bother with a shave and his jaw is stubbled with a five o'clock shadow.

I don't think he likes it though.

Because I always catch him touching it, rubbing and scratching it as if irritated.

A gesture that's more like a habit to him. That he's performing right now even, as he talks to the girl, his face turned toward her, a smirk lurking on his ruby-red lips.

A gesture that makes me think that maybe he likes smooth things. Soft things.

Things like his hoodie.

His white hoodie, to be precise.

So his hoodies are famous around school and in town. They're always white or cream colored and they always seem thick and cozy.

And of course soft.

Also, his hoodies are his favorite thing to wear.

Because he always has them on — well, except in summers but still. That and his dark jeans.

Black and white.

And needless to say, girls around town are obsessed with his hoodies.

They stare at them. They talk about them. They want to touch his hoodies and play with the strings. They want to wear his hoodies too.

Which from what I've heard is a privilege.

Not every girl gets to wear them, only the special ones, and so it's a coveted thing: Reed Roman Jackson and his hoodies.

Even now the girl who's wrapped around him is tracing the fabric, pulling on the strings, fingering the edge of his sleeve at his wrist as she laughs at something he's said.

Stop staring, Callie.

Right.

I need to stop staring. But the thing is that it's very hard to do.

See, that's his magic I think.

The dark magic that I was talking about.

It makes him glow.

Like his very skin absorbs whatever light is in the vicinity, leaving the rest of the world in darkness.

So much so that the only thing you can see, the only thing that you *can* focus on, is him and nothing else.

But.

But, but, but.

I'm one of the Thornes. I'm my brothers' sister. I know better.

So I should look away, and I do.

Well, I try to.

Because the moment I make the decision to look away, *he* decides to look up at me.

And I step back.

As if someone has pushed me. As if *he* has pushed me. He has put his hands on me and I had to step back, *had* to, under the weight of his touch.

The strength of his gaze, his wolf eyes that land right on me.

And now that he has found me, he's not letting me go.

He's absolutely *not* letting me leave. My legs won't even move. They won't.

Because they somehow, the traitors, know that he wants me here.

It's in the way that he slowly straightens up, the way he completely abandons interest in the girl beside him. It's in the way something breaks open on his face, on his gorgeous, *gorgeous* face made up of sharp, smooth, fascinating lines as soon as he sees me.

Something that looks a lot like interest. Curiosity.

Something that makes his pretty eyes go slightly wide followed by a tiny smirk on his lips.

It's like… he's excited that I'm here.

It's like he's thinking, *now the fun begins…*

I'm not sure how I know all of this. But I do.

It's not as if I'm an expert on Reed Roman Jackson.

I mean, we haven't even talked before.

This may be the first time that he's looked at me, and this morning when I woke up, I had no idea that today would be the day he'd look at me for the first time ever.

So yeah, I have no clue how I know all this except that I feel exposed under his eyes. I feel vulnerable and fragile. I feel like I've somehow walked into an evil den.

His evil den.

Which isn't that far from the truth.

I *am* in his evil den and I need to move. Right now.

I need to run. I need to…

Suddenly there's a commotion and Reed's attention breaks away from me. And I think I draw my first breath since he found me in this chaos.

It's Tempest. The source of commotion, I mean. She's running toward Reed.

Yikes.

I'd completely forgotten about her. I don't even know when she broke away from me and made her way through the crowd to go to her brother.

Who definitely looks surprised right now.

He even stands up from his kingly perch just as Tempest launches herself at him. Squealing, she wraps her arms and legs around him and hugs him tight.

And right in front of my eyes, I see a new side of Reed.

A side that hugs his sister back just as tightly. A side that smiles — a true smile — and laughs when his sister moves away and doesn't stop talking. A side that looks at her with a fondness that I've never seen before.

Or rather, that I've only seen on *my* brothers' faces when I surprise them with a new pair of knitted socks or some chocolate chip cookies.

Right in front of my eyes, I discover that Reed Roman Jackson, the gorgeous villain, my brother's rival and enemy, loves his little sister.

Something moves in my chest at this.

Something achy and swollen.

And God, I have to leave now.

I have to.

The longer I stay here, the more restless I feel. The more likely it becomes that someone might recognize me and tell Ledger.

It bugs me to leave Tempest like this because I really like her. But I have to go.

So taking a deep breath and with a last look at Tempest talking to Reed, who's chuckling, I turn around and start walking.

I hunch my shoulders and duck my head, trying to make myself as invisible as possible so no one pays me any attention. Although I'm not sure that I'm walking in the right direction or the direction that I came from.

But it's okay.

I'll find my way out.

So I keep walking, my feet crunching the leaves, until I leave the party behind and get deeper into the trees.

It should be kinda scary to be walking around the woods in the dark. But I grew up here, in this town. Even though I've never really ventured into these woods, I know I'll be safe.

Well, I know that until I hear a noise.

A series of noises actually.

They're not loud or anything. It's just that the woods are quiet and so they *seem* loud. They seem urgent and needy.

And oh my God I come to a halt.

My heart is banging inside my chest. The hairs on the back of my neck are standing up because what the heck is going on?

What…

A twig snaps next. Then a moan comes, followed by heavy breathing.

A second later though when I hear a grunt — a manly grunt — everything becomes clear.

Oh my God.

Someone — a *guy* — is doing something to a girl.

Isn't he?

This is what's happening. A stupid drunk guy is doing something to an innocent girl and I need to go help her.

That's why my brothers are always worried. Because this is what happens at high school parties. Guys drink and go crazy and think they can do whatever they want to a girl.

Well, not on my watch.

He doesn't know what's coming for him.

Me.

I'm coming for him and I know how to punch.

Yeah, that's right. I know how to throw a mean, *mean* punch – four brothers, remember? – and he's getting it.

Right in his face.

Swallowing down my fear, I start to walk toward the

noises.

I'm trying to be as quiet as possible.

I don't want that *animal* to know that I'm coming for him. I'm gonna take him by surprise. That's the best way to do the most damage. That's what my brothers taught me.

But as it turns out, I don't think I'll be using any of the punching skills that I learned from my brothers.

Because there is no drunk guy and no innocent girl.

I mean, he could be drunk and she could be innocent but he's not doing anything to her that she doesn't want. In fact, she seems pretty into it, what he's doing to her. Which is kissing.

He's kissing her and she's kissing him back.

They're standing under a tree and there are a couple of candles around them. A blanket, beers.

Oops.

I think I crashed a date. Which is completely escalating right now.

Now that I'm close and thankfully hiding behind a tree of my own, I can hear more noises. Chuckles, rustling of their clothes, a few murmurs.

And gosh, I can see stuff too.

Their hands and legs and their mouths. It's like they're attacking each other — happily but attacking nonetheless with their lips and limbs.

I don't think I've ever seen anything like this before.

What I mean is that I have seen people kiss before even though I've never been kissed myself. But this is something... else.

This is passion and lust and rawness and holy God, I can't stop looking and I know…

My thoughts break when I hear another noise.

Or rather a *voice*.

I hear a voice.

A voice saying, "You like that, huh?"

It's rich and smooth. *Deep.*

God, so deep.

It makes me think of taking a dive off a skyscraper. It's strange that a voice can invoke such imagery and such a reckless, dangerous image at that. But I swear I feel the rush of air on my body, the adrenaline pumping through my veins as if I'm really flying.

Just because I heard a voice. *His* voice.

It's his. I know.

Even though it has never been directed at me, I've heard it before, and without volition, memorized it. And now it's here.

The voice. *Him.*

And before I can think anything else, assess the situation or even absorb it, I spin around.

As if a string is looped around my body, and he holds the other end. And he's tugging it viciously, making me spin like the ballerina that I am.

And there he is again.

A lot closer to me than he's ever been.

Reed Roman Jackson.

Chapter 3

The first time I saw him, off the soccer field I mean – I'd seen him play plenty of times before that – was my first day at Bardstown High.

It was during my lunch period.

I was trying to find the administration office without having to bother either Ledger or Conrad for every little thing, and despite being given very explicit directions leading to it, I think I took a wrong turn somewhere.

I ended up in a deserted sort of hallway with only a few lingering students in it.

I was trying to find my way back when I stumbled upon an empty classroom.

Well, empty except for two people.

One of which was him.

That was the first time I'd seen him out of his green and white soccer uniform, without sweat dripping from his brows and without a vicious flush covering his features from running across the field.

In fact, it was the first time I'd seen his features clearly and not from a distance.

The first time I'd seen how breathtakingly beautiful he was. How his features, sharp and angled, were designed to make your heart ache as soon as you looked at him.

Heartbreakingly beautiful. That's what I thought in that moment.

Also, tall.

It was something I'd never realized before, his towering frame.

I remember thinking that Reed Roman Jackson was the tallest guy I'd ever seen. Taller than even my brothers, and my brothers are some of the tallest people I know.

In his white hoodie, something else that I saw for the first time, Reed stood leaning against the wall by the whiteboard and God, the top of his head almost reached up to the edge of it. His head was slightly thrown back, exposing the masculine bulge of his Adam's apple and the strained veins running down the side of his neck.

Oh, and his eyes were closed and his jaw was tight.

At first, I didn't get why.

I didn't get why he'd be standing there with his eyes closed like that, his jaw tight before loosening up and his mouth parting on a quiet breath.

At first, I also thought that he was alone.

But then I heard a sound — a moan — and I realized

that there was a girl in the room with him. And she was on her knees, almost hidden by the teacher's desk, in front of him.

That's when I knew.

That the girl he was with was... you know, doing stuff to him. And before I could stop myself, I gasped.

I gasped loudly and as soon as I did, they heard it.

The girl stopped doing stuff to him and a frown appeared between his brows.

To this day, I *know* he was going to open his eyes a second later. And when he did, his gaze would land directly on me. So I ran. I didn't wait for them to figure out that someone was watching them and that it was me.

I ran and saved myself that day.

I don't think I can save myself now.

I don't even think I can run. And it becomes even harder when another moan comes from behind me.

This one particularly loud and needy and like an idiot, *idiot*, I gasp like I did the first time I saw him.

But unlike that time, I'm not hiding behind a door and his eyes aren't closed.

They are open and they are on me and at my gasp, his eyes, those pretty wolf eyes, glint. His lips, ruby-red and plush, tip up slightly too.

And I don't think I've ever felt more exposed in my life.

More seen and vulnerable and trapped and... thrilled, all at the same time, and I think I almost explode with all the jumbled emotions when I hear, "Oh God, Justin. Stop fucking around and put it in already."

And I think *he* knows it.

The guy who's standing in front of me and watching me through all this.

Because out of nowhere he jars every cell in my body when he calls out, "Hey Justin!"

This time I don't even bother stopping myself or castigating myself for doing it, I just *gasp*.

Nor do I stop myself from widening my eyes and questioning him with them: *What are you doing?*

He seems to hear my unspoken question and he answers me in the most non-traditional sense ever.

Without breaking our gaze, he calls out again, "Take it somewhere else." He pauses for a few seconds as squeaks and curses break out. "You're corrupting good little freshman girls."

I wince at his description and his smirk grows.

That was not fair.

I'm *not* a good little freshman girl.

I mean, I am. But he didn't have to say it in such a condescending manner. In a manner that makes me feel like an innocent, inexperienced flower.

Which again, I am, but still.

"Freshman?" A male voice – Justin – answers. "How'd a freshman get in here?"

Reed's mouth twists into a sardonic smile as he answers Justin while still looking at me. "Maybe this year's crop's sneakier than we thought."

This time the girl speaks. "Well, kick them out! They're boring. And God, they're so easily shocked."

My mouth falls open.

That is *not* true.

We're not easily shocked.

Reed finds my reaction highly amusing and a small chuckle escapes him. "Yeah, they are. Aren't they?" I glare at him but that only makes him chuckle once again. "So that's why you need to take your X-rated show somewhere else. Let them dream about birds and bees for one more night."

I'm outraged at this.

Outraged and offended.

Who does he think I am? And why the heck is he talking about me like I'm not even here?

Justin doesn't find it offensive, however. He thinks it's funny, and so does the girl, who giggles and replies, "Hate to break it to you, Reed. But as annoying as freshmen are, I *think* they know how babies are made."

Somehow, his animal eyes grow even more potent and I'm forced to take a step back.

Not that I have anywhere to go really.

My spine is pretty much stuck to the tree I was hiding behind.

And he knows that.

His eyes flick to the ground to gauge the distance between us before lifting back to my face. "Yeah? Well, this one looks a little too daisy fresh. I'm not sure she can handle your sex ed class without passing out. So fuck off."

I think I just pulled a muscle.

Because this is the hardest that I've frowned and glared

and pursed my lips at someone, the hardest and the longest.

Meanwhile his friends, who still don't know that I'm standing here, listening in, chuckle and laugh and make crude comments from behind me.

When they're done though, they scramble off.

Leaving me alone with him.

The guy who's staring at me like I'm the most interesting thing he has seen tonight. The most interesting thing he's ever seen, actually, and now that I'm in his clutches, he can't wait to play with me.

He can't wait to open me up, unravel me, take me apart.

He can't *wait*.

"I'm not daisy fresh," I say and regret it soon after.

This is what I say to him, *this*.

Of all the things I could've said, like *how dare you talk about me while I was standing right here* or *how dare you sneak up on me* — because he did sneak up on me, right? — I say the most asinine thing ever.

I go to take it back.

But no words come out of my mouth because he chooses that very moment to move his eyes.

Which makes me realize that he hasn't looked anywhere else except my face ever since he got here.

He's changing that now though.

He's slowly making his way down my swallowing, hiccupping throat, my heavily breathing chest.

Even though there's very little light, I know he can see me clearly.

I think it's his wolf eyes; they can see in the dark.

They can see everything: my cardigan that I knitted my-self – it's early February and unusually un-winter-like weather that only requires a light sweater – and my dress.

When his eyes move over it, I realize something else too.

Something both silly and important.

Daisies.

I'm wearing daisies.

My dress has printed daisies on it. That's why he said that.

Oh, and it's white, my dress.

Holy crap.

Lost in the woods, I'm dressed in his favorite color — white — and he's staring at me in a way that makes him look like a predator. Part human, part wolf, who hunts unsuspecting girls like me.

Girls foolish enough to wander alone at midnight.

"I beg to differ," he drawls when he finishes his perusal and comes back up to my face. "You look daisy fresh to me."

See?

Predator.

Beautiful, gorgeous… predator.

I fist my dress and press my back into the tree. Raising my chin, I try to look more experienced even though I'm any-thing but. "And I'm not a freshman either."

"Is that so?"

Look at that tone, so condescending.

God, I hate him.

Also, I hate myself for saying that.

But now that I have, I'm going to stay the course, because backing down would be even more cowardly.

"Yes," I tell him. "I mean I am. But I should've been a sophomore. I repeated a year. And so I'm older and hence wiser. I'm about to turn sixteen in three months."

All true.

I did repeat a year. Back when my mom had been sick and eventually died of cancer.

Everything had fallen on Conrad, who was only eighteen at the time and a freshman in college. He had so many, *many* balls to juggle back then, what with my mom's deteriorating health, getting a job, keeping the house, taking care of my brothers and me – well, all my brothers chipped in and helped with me, but they were all kids themselves – that perfect attendance wasn't very high on the list.

So my teachers thought it would be best if I repeated a year.

"Sweet sixteen, huh," he murmurs, his eyes all glowy and intense.

I swallow. "Yes. So you shouldn't have said what you said. To your friends."

"What'd I say to my friends?"

I fist my dress harder.

I know what he's doing. He's provoking me. Because this is what he does.

He, Reed Roman Jackson, provokes and I, Calliope Juliet Thorne, make good choices.

So I should make a good choice here and backtrack.

But something in his eyes, in his casual but also tight demeanor, makes me say, "That I don't know."

"You don't know what?"

I lick my dry lips. "That I don't know how babies are made."

"And how *are* they made?"

Stop. Just stop, Callie.

But you know what, I hate that he's so amused right now.

It makes me want to say it, throw him off, shock him.

So I widen my stance and throw back my shoulders as I say, "They are made when you f-fuck."

What?

What did I say?

Oh God.

I think I've shocked myself. I've never ever said that word before, never.

I've heard it though. A million times. I have four brothers, of course I've heard it. But I've never said it.

Not until tonight.

Not until *he* made me say it.

The guy who has gone slightly still. Like he wasn't expecting me to take the bait.

Well, good.

There. That'll teach him not to underestimate me.

"Is that the first time you've said that word?" he asks mockingly, with his eyes narrowed.

I hate that he makes me feel so breathless and young.

"Why, are you proud that you made me say that word for the first time?"

His jaw moves, that stubbled, sharp thing. It tics for a moment before he says, "Not particularly, no."

"Well –"

"Don't ever say it again."

"What?"

"It doesn't suit you."

I'm so confused.

Did he just… tell me not to say the F word?

He did, didn't he?

But that's…

Who is *he* to tell me that? Who is he to tell me anything?

"Yeah, I don't think you can tell me what I can or can't say," I tell him, raising my eyebrows, which only makes his jaw tic even more. "And while we're at it, you shouldn't have talked about me with your friends like I wasn't here. That's bad manners."

"What about crashing someone's party? Does that also fall under bad manners?" he shoots back.

My lips part.

Okay, he got me.

I *am* crashing his party. I wasn't really invited, was I?

"I wasn't… I was leaving," I say. "I just got lost."

"Lost."

"Yes."

His eyes glow again and something flashes through his features that I don't really understand. "You do that a lot, don't you? Get lost."

"I don't... what?"

"In the woods. In the hallways..."

He leaves that sentence hanging but I get his meaning. I get it and oh my God.

He knows.

He knows it was me. That I saw him. Months and months ago, on my first day at Bardstown High.

He *knows.*

A rush of heat fans over my cheeks. My throat, my entire body actually, and can I just dissolve into this tree?

Can I just please disappear?

"I'm... I didn't think you..."

"Knew?" He smirks. "I did."

"But I was... quiet."

"You weren't as quiet as you think you were. Besides..."

"Besides what?"

He leans forward slightly, the strings of his hoodie swinging, as if confessing a secret. "I didn't mind. Being watched by you. The Thorn Princess. And if you hadn't run away, I would've gotten rid of her."

"You would have?"

"Yeah."

"W-why?"

"So I could focus all my attention." Then, with a lowered voice, "On you."

My heart bangs against my ribs, bruising them. Battering them, making them throb.

In fact, my whole body throbs.

I can feel it. I can *hear* it even.

Even so, I try to hold on to my composure. I try to hold on to the authority in my voice. "As if."

"As if what?"

"As if I would've... let you or even stayed."

"I think you would've." He keeps his gaze steady and unwavering, both intense and slightly amused. "And I think you would've enjoyed it too. Girls love it when I give them my attention. They're known to even beg for it. On their knees particularly."

My knees tingle at that as if zapped by a current. They buckle too.

As if they're going to bend. As if I'm going to fall.

But I won't.

"I'm not like other girls," I tell him. "I don't beg."

Something about that makes him smirk. "Every girl begs. She just needs the right thing to beg for."

I narrow my eyes at him. "My brothers would kill you."

I'm the Thorn Princess, as he said.

That's what they call me. I'm the princess, the little sister of four legendary soccer gods who so completely hate him.

"I think I can handle myself," he says, all casual like.

"You should be afraid of my brothers, you know."

"Why is that?"

"There's four of them and only one of you."

"So?"

"So you shouldn't talk to me this way."

He gives me a once-over before asking in an amused voice, "Why, does it make you want to beg me for something?"

"It doesn't –"

"You shouldn't worry about me too much. As I said, I can handle myself."

I think so too.

He looks so cavalier, so fearless. *Reckless.*

My brothers could crush him if they wanted to.

My brothers could crush *any* guy if they wanted to and everyone in this town knows that. Everyone in Bardstown is afraid of them.

Not him though.

Not Reed Roman Jackson.

He never was and he never will be.

I mean, look at what just happened on the field. What happens every time on the field and also off it. And before I can stop myself, I ask, "Why do you hate Ledger so much?"

"Who says I hate him?"

"You're always fighting with him, provoking him. Like you did today. On the field."

"So you were watching, huh?" he murmurs instead.

"Of course. I watch every game. For Ledger. And for Con."

He stares at me for a beat before chuckling softly. "Of course. Well, your *brother* makes it easy. To provoke."

"Why can't you just get along? You're on the same team."

"You tell him to quit the team and we will."

"He's the captain," I tell him like he doesn't know.

"Not for long."

"What is that supposed to mean?"

He shrugs, his mountain-like shoulders rising and falling. "It means that he must be getting tired."

"Of what?"

"Of doing a shitty job of it. Of losing to his forward."

Right.

Of course.

The stupid contest.

So after Reed provoked Ledger, he lost his head for a while and in that while, Reed scored and won their contest, along with winning the game.

"Your *team* won," I say, exasperated. "So he didn't lose. And neither did you."

"You're right, I didn't."

"You know it's a stupid contest, right? It doesn't mean anything," I say.

He nods sagely. "Yeah, you should say that to your brother. It might help him sleep tonight. After losing, I mean."

I study him a beat, all proud and handsome.

Arrogant.

A wrecking ball really.

"Is winning that important to you?"

"Winning is everything," he replies gravely.

"And what about team spirit?"

"Fuck team spirit."

"And love of the game?"

He scoffs. "Yeah, the only thing I love is being the best.

And my Mustang. I love that too."

Oh, his Mustang.

How did I forget about that?

The other reason why people call him the Wild Mustang is because he owns one. A Mustang, the car. Obviously in white, and rumor has it that he loves it.

It's his most precious possession.

Which is why one time, Ledger and guys from the Thorn camp slashed his tires before an important game, just to mess with Reed, and I have to admit that I didn't like that.

I felt bad for Reed.

But then I found out that Ledger did it in retaliation against Reed sleeping with a girl he liked, again before a big game, to mess with Ledger's head.

So yeah, that killed my sympathy.

"Your Mustang," I repeat in a flat voice.

"Yeah. It goes from zero to sixty faster than a girl can strip. What's not to love?"

I'm... disappointed.

I don't know why.

I mean, it's not something that I didn't expect.

For years, Ledger has been telling me the same thing. He's been telling me that Reed doesn't care about the team. That Reed is selfish. He only looks out for himself.

Conrad has been saying it too.

That's why he picked Ledger as the captain instead of Reed. Even though they're both excellent. Even though Reed's even better on some occasions.

So I've got no clue why I'm disappointed at hearing this from his own mouth when I already knew what his answer was going to be.

Reed Roman Jackson is exactly what they told me he'd be.

A villain.

Sighing, I duck my head. "I'm leaving."

I don't even manage to take a step before he says, "Not so fast."

My head snaps up. "What?"

As if that wasn't jarring enough, him stopping me, he decides to make me hyperventilate by starting to approach me.

So far we've been standing at a respectable, comfortable distance. Like twelve feet or so. But now he's closing that distance, one step at a time.

Each swing of his legs is almost a foot long and makes the powerful muscles in his thighs bulge. Makes his boots crush the leaves noisily.

I press myself to the tree as I watch him approach me. As I watch him watch me.

He knows I'm afraid.

I can see it on his features.

His beautifully relaxed mouth, the lines of satisfaction around his eyes.

"What are you doing?" I ask, my fingers digging into the bark of the tree.

He stops probably one arm away, so solid and towering, as he muses, "I'm assuming your brothers don't know that you're here."

His low voice makes me swallow. "Why?"

"Just a hunch." He dips his chin toward me, bringing us ever so slightly closer, as he smiles, sort of evilly. "And I also think they're not going to like the fact that you've wandered into the enemy camp."

I'm not sure if it's his nearness or what but I think that every part of his body is dangerous. That his blade-like cheekbones could cut and his teeth could rip.

His fingers could squeeze and hurt and that he could somehow make me like all of that.

He could make me *like* the way he'd hurt me.

I raise my chin, trying to look brave. "Are you going to tell them?"

Those sharp teeth of his come out to play when he smiles again. "Now that's an interesting thought, isn't it?"

"Please don't," I blurt out before I can stop myself. "As I said, I was leaving. You don't have to say anything. You could just… keep this between us."

Great. Just great, Callie.

Tell the villain that you want him to keep a secret.

As expected, his eyes glow.

Like he was waiting for me to slip up.

Like he was waiting for me to fall into his trap and only God can save me now.

Maybe not even Him because when he speaks in a low, raspy voice I have to press my legs together as his words drop down and sit somewhere low, very low in my stomach.

"What do I get in return? If I keep it." He tilts his head to the side. "Between us."

Run, I tell myself.

Just please push him away and start running.

But all I do is stand here, staring up at him, even when it becomes difficult, even when it strains my neck because he's so tall and big.

So beautiful that I don't know where else to look.

I also don't know how to stop myself from asking, "W-what do you want?"

This is what he wanted, isn't it?

Yeah, because his features grow warm with satisfaction before he drawls, "You."

"What?"

Slowly, those eyes of his travel all the way down to my white ballet flats. "I hear you're a ballerina."

My right foot tries to climb on to my left under his scrutiny. "Yes."

He lifts his eyes. "Then I want you to spin like one."

"I-I'm sorry?"

He shifts on his feet, making himself bigger somehow, pushing at the very fabric of the air, as he explains, "You like to dance, don't you? So I want you to dance. For me."

I blink at him.

I think I heard him wrong. He cannot possibly be asking what I think he's asking.

Just to be sure, I question, "You want me to dance for you?"

"Yeah."

"In exchange for you keeping this between us?"

"That's the idea."

My mouth falls open. "You're insane."

"I'd like to think of myself as someone who sees an opportunity and seizes it."

"What opportunity?"

"I was bored and then a ballerina fell into my lap. A good one too, from what I've heard." Again, he gives me a once-over. "So I want you to entertain me."

I ignore the flush of pleasure at his off-handed compliment. Mostly because it's *off-handed* and followed by a very presumptuous demand.

And also because, as I said, he's insane.

"What do you think this is?" I ask, exasperated. "A movie from the fifties or something? Where you're a cigar-smoking villain and you're blackmailing me into dancing for you."

"A cigar-smoking villain." He's amused. "I'm known to smoke a cigarette here and there and I usually prefer the term asshole but I like that. It has a certain flair to it."

"I'm not going to dance for you."

"Well then, I'm going to enjoy watching Ledger lose his shit in the next game when I tell him how pretty his sister looked, standing before me, begging me to keep her secret."

I clench my teeth in anger.

Have I said that I hate him?

I really, really do.

"Fine. *Fine*," I snap at him. "I'll dance for you. But just for making me do that, you also have to apologize to my brother."

"Apologize."

"Yes. You provoked him on the field today. I don't know what you said but you're going to apologize to him when you see him next."

A flash of irritation tightens his mouth. "Just so you know, I don't do well with orders."

I go up on my tiptoes then.

Because he's so tall and I want to get up in his face, which of course he notices, my feet arched up and my calves strained.

And something in my struggle to appear all strong in front of him turns his gaze even more molten.

"Well, you're gonna have to start," I tell him, "because I'm not dancing until you promise me."

He watches me silently for a few moments before stepping back.

And I think it's over.

I've called his bluff.

But then, he fishes something out of his back pocket, his cell phone, and presses a few buttons on the screen.

Suddenly, the music that was a dull sound in the background flares to life. The air fills with heavy bass and people back at the party cheer.

He commands in a husky voice, "Make it good."

Just like that, he's called *my* bluff and I'm supposed to dance for him.

How did this happen? How is this my life?

When I woke up this morning all I wanted to do was get

through my classes, go to the game, and go back home to the scarf that I'm knitting for Conrad.

But somehow, I'm here, about to dance for my brother's rival.

That's not the worst part.

The worst part is that I want to.

I *want* to dance for him.

I've been *wanting* to dance for him ever since I saw him play for the first time three years ago. When both he and Ledger made the team.

God.

I'm so embarrassed to admit that. So ashamed.

But the thing is that the way he plays soccer, the way he moves across the field, with grace and beauty and a certain recklessness, fills me with music.

Not to mention, the music that he's put on... is gorgeous.

It's a mix of hip hop and rock and when the word *ballerina* flutters in the air, I let go of the tree that I've been clinging to and step forward.

When the guy in the song calls me his – his ballerina – it feels like *he's* calling me that.

The Wild Mustang who's asked me to dance for him.

And when the guy follows it up with how his ballerina drops her body like a stripper, I have to lick my dried lips and wipe my sweaty hands on my dress.

I should be offended – this song reeks of dirty, filthy sex – but I'm not.

I'm not even nervous.

There isn't the slightest bit of hesitation in me.

My body is buzzing with excitement, with shooting stars, and when I close my eyes for a second, I see light behind my eyelids.

I can't see anything on his face though.

It's expressionless, tight.

But when I take a deep breath and raise my arms, his features change.

They become somehow sharper and more chiseled but also fluid.

I think it's his lips that part slightly when I take my first spin and his eyes that shine like diamonds when I begin to sway my hips to the beat.

And after that my eagerness to dance for him knows no bounds.

I'm dying, actually *dying*, to spin for him, to sway and move.

To rock my hips and bite my lips.

To look him in his wolf eyes that grow alert with my every leap and jump. More on edge.

In fact, his whole body seems on edge, excited even.

His whole body moves to keep me in sight as I circle around him.

His feet spin when I do.

His fists clench when I throw my arms in the air.

His mouth parts when mine does to take in a shaky breath.

God.

Reed Roman Jackson is just as eager as me.

Just as tightly wound and I've never seen him this way.

I've never seen him *excited* for anything.

The knowledge of that, the knowledge that his heart might be racing just as fast as my heart and that the beads of sweat on his forehead match the beads of sweat on mine, makes me dizzy.

It makes me drunk and drugged and so high on his attention that when the song crescendos and I do my last spin, I stumble.

The world tips and I lose my balance. The ground seems to have vanished from under my feet and I have no choice but to fall.

He catches me at the last second though.

His arm goes around my waist and instead of crashing down to the ground, I go crashing into his body. My hands land on his ribs and my fingers clutch onto his hoodie.

A thousand thoughts, a thousand sensations, explode in my mind, but the very first that jumps out is that it's soft.

His hoodie.

It's the softest, coziest, plushest thing I've ever touched. Even more than the sweaters that I knit for my brothers.

The thought that immediately follows is that no wonder he loves it, his hoodie.

No wonder he wears it all the time, because everything else about him is hard and harsh and sharp.

His strong arm that's wrapped around my waist. The power in his thighs that are pressed against my stomach.

Panting and looking up into his animal eyes, I whisper, "I know that it might not matter, coming from me, but…" I swallow, gripping his hoodie tighter, my brain foggy and my tongue spewing words I don't understand. "But I think you're amazing. O-on the field, I mean. You're just so gorgeous and reckless and feral, the way you… play. It's no wonder that they call you the Wild Mustang. It's no wonder…"

I trail off, embarrassed.

What the heck am I saying?

Why am I telling him this?

I shouldn't. These are my private thoughts. *Traitor* thoughts that I shouldn't even entertain.

"No wonder what?" he rasps, his strong, muscled arm squeezing my waist.

I can't stop the words from tumbling out of my mouth then. "No wonder why girls can't stop watching you."

No wonder why I can't stop watching you.

A blush fans over my cheeks as soon as I say it and I lower my eyes.

"It does," he says.

I look up. "What?"

He squeezes my waist again. "It matters. Coming from you."

"Oh."

"And you're not a princess."

"I'm not?"

He shakes his head slowly, his eyes all intense and piercing. "You're a fairy."

I lick my lips then and his wolf eyes flare and I open my tingling mouth to say something — not sure what — when there's a shout.

"Jackson!"

My eyes pop wide at that voice and my fingers in his hoodie tighten even more.

Because I know it. I know that voice too.

It belongs to someone I know and someone I love and someone I'm completely betraying by being here.

My brother, Ledger.

Chapter 4

My brother is here.

Somehow, he's found me, and I'm wrapped around the guy he hates the most.

The guy who should be worried right now.

Very, very worried.

But he's not.

He's sweeping his eyes over my face as if memorizing it before he smiles slightly and steps back, easily getting out of my grip.

My fingers feel empty without his hoodie but I don't have the time to dwell on it because I hear Ledger again.

"Get the fuck away from her."

At this, I finally gather my wits and turn to look at my brother.

He's charging at us, rage flickering over his features.

Like Reed, my brother is tall, not *quite* as tall as Reed,

and is muscled and strong. He's slightly wider in the shoulders and chest than Reed, and with the way he's glaring at Reed, I feel like he's going to use his size to his advantage.

But I really wish that this was it.

That the threat of Ledger practically bulldozing Reed, who believe it or not *still* does not look worried about it at all, was the only threat to contend with.

It's not, though.

Because I have not one but four brothers, and somehow, they're *all* here.

All of them.

How are they here? How did they know where to find me?

Even the two who're supposed to be away at college, Stellan and Shepard, the twins.

They're identical to each other and are also tall – again, not as tall as Reed – and built like Ledger, slightly wider in the chest and shoulders.

The biggest one though is my oldest brother, Conrad.

He's the tallest – definitely as tall as Reed – and the broadest too.

He isn't charging the scene like the other three but walking with authority, with a purpose that's even scarier than the pure rage radiating out of the others.

That's what makes me break into action and step in front of Reed.

"Ledger, stop," I say, raising my arms.

He's still a few feet away from us and at my voice, he

finally focuses on me. "What the fuck are you doing? Get away from him, Callie."

"Ledge, I –"

"Did he do something to you?" he spits out before glancing back at the object of his hatred, standing behind me. "Why the fuck were you wrapped around him? Tell me he didn't touch you."

I shake my head. "No, he didn't –"

"Or what?" Reed says from behind me, his voice a mixture of amused and provoking.

"Or we can turn this into one of the more fun nights than we've had in a while." That's Shepard, who stops right beside Ledger and shrugs casually.

"Fun for us. Just FYI. Not sure if it would be fun for you but still." This comes from Stellan — he's the more serious twin — who comes to stand right beside Shepard.

I can't believe they're here, Stellan and Shep.

They're supposed to be in New York. In college. Nobody told me that they were coming home this weekend.

God, what are they doing here?

Even though they're all standing right in front of me, I *still* can't believe that my four overprotective older brothers somehow figured out that I'm here.

Instead of where I told them I'd be.

See, this is what happens when you lie, Callie.

Not to mention, they all look intimidating like this, making a wall of muscles and dark glares.

They're all almost the same height and build and they all

have thick, dark hair and brown eyes except for Conrad.

His hair's dirty blond with a few golden strands and his eyes are dark blue.

He's the brother I'm closest to in appearance and he's the brother I'm most afraid of. Maybe because he's more like a father figure than an older brother.

Although right now, I'm afraid of every single one of them.

Not Reed, apparently.

Because he walks closer to them, thereby rendering the meager protection I was giving him moot. "Well then, you've come to the right place. Let the fun begin."

And from the looks of it, the fun is definitely going to begin because a crowd has gathered around us.

Someone has turned off the music and most of the people have made sort of a semi-circle around us. They're still at a distance, but they're definitely watching.

Great. Just great.

My brothers don't care about that though.

Reed's cavalier words have made them frown and they each take a threatening step toward him.

Except Conrad.

Conrad, who stands a little farther away from the rest of my brothers, says, "Callie, come here."

I breathe heavily, glancing from my three ready-to-fight brothers to my oldest one. "Con, please. He didn't do anything."

"Callie."

"He didn't –"

"Get over here."

I wince and start walking toward him. And as soon as I do, the rest of my brothers shift and sort of make a boundary out of their bodies, a line between me and the rest of the world, *him* more specifically, in a very obvious display of protectiveness.

As soon as I reach Conrad, I tell him, "Please, Con. He didn't do anything. I promise and –"

"You lied," he says.

Not loudly or bitterly or in anger.

He says it in a matter-of-fact way and my heart twists.

It's not as if I've never lied to my brothers. Of course I have, but this is something big. Something serious. I know that.

As I said, they only have one rule: they need to know where I am at all times. So they know that I'm safe.

They give me everything that I ask for.

Even though they can be controlling and dominating – as evidenced by this display – they try to be reasonable. They try to understand where I'm coming from. They respect my freedom.

So I'm at fault here.

"I'm sorry," I whisper.

Conrad's chest pushes out on a breath and instead of anger, there's disappointment. "Let's go home."

I look at my three angry brothers, who still appear ready to fight, and turn to Conrad. "I'm sorry. I'm sorry that I lied. Just please tell them not to fight. H-he didn't do anything."

At this, I see anger though.

I do see his broad features going tight. "Come on."

"But Con –"

"Not a word right now."

I snap my mouth shut.

Then glancing over my shoulders, Conrad calls out, "Just one. No more."

I don't know what that means or which brother he's talking to.

Until I hear a thump and a crunch. And loud gasps and murmurs from the crowd.

At which point, I spin around and see that Ledger has punched Reed in the face, and Reed's wiping his mouth with the back of his hand, somehow with his smirk still in place.

And he's *bleeding*.

Oh God.

Despite everything I try to go to him, but Con grabs my arm, stopping me.

Thankfully though, there's someone else out here who cares about him.

His sister, Tempest.

She breaks away from the crowd and dashes over to her brother who in turn does the same thing my brothers are doing to me: he frowns at her first before sort of stepping in front of her as if to say that the world will have to go through him in order to get to her.

My heart squeezes again at this brotherly display of protectiveness, this whole other side of Reed Roman Jackson.

And I'm embarrassed that his sister is witnessing all this hatred, but at least she's here for him. Also now she *really* knows how bad the blood is between my brothers and hers.

When our eyes clash, I mouth, *sorry*.

She smiles sadly and mouths, *my fault*.

Well, not really.

I mean she didn't put a gun to my head to bring me here. She insisted and I agreed. I could've said no and avoided this whole debacle.

But apparently not.

Anyway my brothers aren't satisfied with one punch. Because all three of them take a step toward him, but Con puts a stop to that.

"Enough. Let's go."

They hate it, of course.

But they don't disobey him.

Out of habit, I guess.

He's not only my father figure, he's theirs too.

He's the one person who's stayed for us. Who's protected us and loved us, fought to keep us together and be our guardian.

He's the reason we're still a family.

So they back off and I breathe out a sigh of relief.

But when the time comes to walk away, I look at *him*.

I look at Reed.

I've been avoiding looking at him directly. I've only thrown him passing glances ever since my brothers got here – I still don't know how – and they caught me in his arms.

But now I look at him.

Only to find that he's looking back.

That his wolf eyes glint and shine as much as his split lip that's bleeding.

I don't know what I see in his gaze but whatever it is makes my heart spin in my chest. Makes it race and pound and squeeze.

This is it, isn't it?

I'm never gonna see him again.

Well, I will see him at school but I'll never *see* him like I did tonight. Or talk to him or be near him or touch his hoodie.

I'll never dance for him either.

I bite my lip at the thought.

The *rogue* thought.

I shouldn't want to anyway but I do.

I do and I…

"Hey, Ledger!"

For the second time tonight, Reed jars the breath out of me when he calls out, this time to my brother, while still keeping his eyes on me.

Ledger, who had started to walk away, comes to a halt and turns around to face him.

Reed isn't alone anymore. Along with Tempest – who's staring at Ledger with wide gray eyes – others from the crowd have joined him now.

And I fist my hands at my sides as I hope and wish and pray that this isn't going to get out of hand.

"I'm sorry," Reed says, jerking his chin at him.

"For fucking what?"

"That you lost tonight." Then, "Even though you deserved it."

Around me, my brothers seethe and I watch some of the

players from the Mustang camp snicker.

But Ledger still obeys Conrad's rule and simply flips him the finger before turning around and striding away.

But I can't move.

Because Reed is back to looking at me.

His wolf eyes home in on me for a few seconds before doing a final sweep of my body and then looking away as he's submerged by the crowd.

And I realize that he kept his promise, didn't he?

The one I forced him to make before I danced for him.

He apologized to my brother.

***

It was someone from the party who told.

Someone from the party who texted someone else. Who in turn texted another someone else and that's how Ledger got the news about where I was.

He tried to call me first.

To confirm, I think. Because he gave me the benefit of the doubt, but when I didn't pick up and when the friend that I'd used as an alibi told him that she never saw me after school ended yesterday, he got pissed.

I'm guessing Conrad came along to calm Ledger down and to rein in the situation if it got out of hand. He's been a witness to many such situations over the years he's been coaching the two.

And when my other two brothers, who were trying to

surprise us with a weekend visit, found out where I was, they came along in case Ledger needed reinforcements.

At least that's what I'm guessing from past experiences – Ledger is the youngest brother and like they are with me, our older brothers are protective of him as well. Not that they'd tell him or that Ledger would like that since he's all grown up and everything but still.

Anyway, they never told me why or what except how they found out where I was.

They never told me anything actually.

Last night when I tried to say something as soon as we reached home, they didn't let me either.

Con told me to go get some sleep and the rest of them just dispersed without having a conversation with me.

Now it's morning and they're still not talking.

Con is shut up in his study and we all know not to disturb him when he's working. One of the ground rules he set up for us when he quit college to come back and take over everything.

The rest of my brothers, I have no idea about.

They're not home.

So I'm upstairs in my room, trying to get my homework done before my ballet class in the afternoon.

But ugh, I can't focus.

They won't even let me apologize to them. They won't even talk to me. They won't even...

There's a knock on the door and I sit up straight; I've been lounging around in my bed with my books spread out in front of me, but now I close them, cross my legs and call out,

"Yeah?"

The door opens and I see Con.

He's got a slight frown on his forehead as he says, sort of roughly, "Hey."

"Hey," I say eagerly.

"You got a second?"

"Yes. Yes, absolutely."

I say this with even more eagerness and my oldest brother, who is so freaking tall that he has to slightly hunch his shoulders to get inside my room, enters.

Without volition, my mind goes to *him*.

My mind goes to the fact that he's just as tall, isn't he?

Would he also have to hunch his mountain-like shoulders to get inside my childhood bedroom?

God, Callie. Not now.

I'm all ready to beat my stupid thoughts into submission but I don't have to. They vanish on their own because as soon as Con enters and moves away from the doorway, I see the rest of my brothers.

They were hovering behind him and one by one, they enter too.

First Stellan, who almost has to hunch but not quite. Then Shepard, who enters with a slight grimace on his face because he thinks my room is too pink for his manliness, and finally, the brother who's closest to me in age and hence has always been my best buddy, Ledger.

It takes them a few seconds to situate themselves around my room and from experience I already know where they're all going to end up before they do.

Ledger leans against my desk, which is located by the white door. Shepard, the noisiest one, drags my desk chair out, spins it around and sits on it backwards with his arms on the backrest.

Stellan goes to stand by my window on the far side of the room. And the reason he does that is because Con is going to sit on the armchair right beside it, which he does a second later, and Stellan is Con's right hand.

Maybe because Stellan is the second oldest – three minutes older than his twin Shepard – and so Con has always trusted him the most. Even though Stellan and Shepard are eight years younger than Con.

When they're all situated and are still not talking, I open my mouth to apologize but I notice Shep elbowing Ledger and as if waking up, Ledger mutters, "Right."

He brings something out from behind him and offers it to me.

It's a giant baby pink box with satin pink ribbon wrapped around it and despite everything, my arms shoot up to grab it.

On the top in a darker shade of pink, is written *Buttery Blossoms*.

It's my favorite, *favorite* bakery in town and they have the best cupcakes ever.

In fact, I even have a picture of it, my most favorite cupcake from there – Peanut Butter Blossom —taped up on my wall.

I have pictures of all my favorite things taped up on my wall actually. My ballet recitals, my pointe shoes, Bardstown

High.

Excitedly, I look at Ledger and then all my brothers. "You guys bought me cupcakes?"

Ledger shrugs. "Yeah."

Shep shrugs too. "They're your favorite."

"And you don't get to have them enough, so," Ledger adds.

That's true, I don't.

Mostly because I'm a ballerina and I have to watch my weight. Healthy living and healthy eating and all that but oh my God, I have a giant addiction to these.

It's toxic but I don't care.

I hug the box, my heart feeling full. "Is that where you guys went this morning? Because I was looking for all of you."

Shep is first to reply with his hands in the air. "I will not set foot in that pink shop. Under any circumstances, so no. I went to see a friend."

Before I can reply, Ledger rolls his eyes. "By that, he means Amy."

My eyes pop wide. "You guys are back together again?"

Amy is Shep's on-again off-again girlfriend from high school and I really, *really* like her. She loves dancing and knitting just like me and I would love to see them end up together.

But Shep is an idiot and he broke up with her when he left for college three years ago.

I always feel bad when I see her around town; she's still so in love with him.

"Fuck no," Shep says.

"Why not? She's amazing, Shep. I really like her."

"Never said I don't like her." He smirks then. "I like her. I like her a lot."

"Yeah, her and that hot tub in her backyard." Ledger snickers.

Shep's smirk only grows. "Oh yeah, definitely. It's got jet sprays, dude. You can't compete with that. That hot tub can do things you can't even fathom, little brother."

"Oh, I can fathom. I can fathom a lot." Ledger playfully kicks at the legs of the chair Shep is sitting in. "In fact, I fathomed it last week with her little sister, Jessica."

Shep turns to Ledger then. "For real? You and –"

But before he can go on, I squeal, "Ew, gross. Both of you."

While at the same time, Stellan speaks up. "Enough. All right? You can exchange your glorious war stories later."

Ugh.

They're such players.

Sometimes I think that's why they hate Reed so much. Because they know he's exactly like them.

Ledger and Shep shut up and before anyone can say anything else and sidetrack the conversation again, I ask, "Why are you guys bringing me cupcakes?"

Ledger side-eyes Stellan and Con. "Because you're our sister."

Getting serious, Shepard nods. "And we love you."

"We also respect you," Ledger says.

"And your choices." Shep goes next.

"Also your independence," Ledger adds, making me think that they've memorized their lines.

Shepard proves me right in the next second. "Yeah, we respect that too." Then frowning, he tilts his head toward Stellan. "Wait, is that what it is? We respect her independence." Looking at me, he explains, "*Stella* here said something this morning that totally went over my hungover head."

Ledger snickers again at *Stella*, I'm sure.

It's my fault really.

When I was a kid, I couldn't say Stellan so I'd call him Stella and, well, it caught on. And now every time Shep wants to annoy Stellan, he calls him Stella.

I glance at Stellan apologetically, who's watching Shep with a flat look. "You like your face, don't you?"

Shepard chuckles because they're identical twins. "Not on you though."

"Yeah, keep talking and I'll rearrange it for you." He glances at Ledger who's still snickering. "Yours too."

When the most mischievous of my brothers, Shep and Ledger, go quiet again – not happily though – Stellan speaks up, looking at me. "Look, what these morons are trying to say is that we acted like giant asses last night. We shouldn't have barged in, like an army or something. But you scared us, all right? It's not like you to lie and we thought something happened to you. We thought –"

Ledger bursts out then, as if he's been holding it all on the inside. "We thought he did something, okay? We thought you needed our help." He shakes his head angrily. "You needed us to rescue you from him and…" He goes quiet for a second before saying, "You need to be careful."

"I know and I am. And –"

"No, it's… you need to be really careful. *Really*."

"O-kay," I say, frowning at Ledger's grave tone. "I am."

"You don't get it." He sighs sharply. "The thing is… fuck it. The thing is that he's attractive. Good looking, handsome, whatever. Not more than me, but still."

"What?" I'm so confused.

Shepard snorts.

Stellan's lips twitch as well.

"Yeah, and also the thing is, Calls, that our little brother wants to say that he's got a big boy crush on him," Shep adds with raised eyebrows.

Stellan chuckles as Ledger swats Shep's head. "Fuck you, dude. I'm trying to explain something."

"No need. We get it," Shepard says, hitting Ledger in the stomach with his elbow.

"The point I'm trying to make is, he takes advantage of that," Ledger continues loudly, rubbing his stomach. "Of his looks. Girls become stupid when it comes to him and he uses their stupidity against them. And you're my sister. He's bound to mess with you. Because he's smart enough to know that I'm going to win this season. Like last season. So you need to stay away from him, Callie. He's a fucking asshole, all right?"

I bite my lip as I finally get my window to apologize. "I know and I'm sorry. I don't want to ruin your game and –"

"This is not about the soccer rivalry."

That's Conrad's voice.

He's been sitting in his spot, all quiet so far, letting the rest of them talk and joke around. But I guess his patience is running thin now, because he pins Shep and Ledger with a hard gaze before turning to me and leaning forward, putting his elbows on his thighs. "I can tolerate a lot. I *have* tolerated a lot over the years. Rebellions, phases, tantrums. But I will not tolerate lies that involve your safety."

He pauses for his words to take effect, and they do.

Because he has.

Tolerated, I mean. A lot.

Obviously from Shepard and Ledger, who are the more rebellious of the bunch. All the times Shepard was suspended from school for playing a prank or making out with girls in the school closets. All the times Ledger got into trouble with his anger. Even Stellan has had his moments, not as frequent or severe as the other two, but still.

And then there's me.

I'm a girl.

A whole different species for my brothers to understand, but they've done their best.

Especially Conrad.

All the times I cried because of ballet and how I wasn't good enough. How even though I love ballet, it didn't leave me enough time to make friends and so I was always excluded from fun sleepovers and tea parties. So all my brothers would entertain me at home, play with me, drink imaginary tea with me.

Not to mention all the things a girl goes through.

That Conrad never even thought about before but had to because we had no one else to turn to.

Tampons and bras and hormones and serious talks about puberty and sex.

So he *has* tolerated a lot.

And I hate that I lied to him.

"We might have come down on you harder than we thought," he continues, his serious dark blue gaze on me. "But it was because we were worried. As Stellan said, it's not like you to lie and I'd like to think that I've given you enough freedom that you don't *have* to lie."

"I know, Con," I say, contrite. "You have. I was scared that you'd be mad if I told you I was going to his party and –"

"Fuck yeah, we would be," Ledger cuts me off.

Con glances at him. "Ledge."

Ledger quiets down then and Con turns back to me. "The reason we don't want you to go to his party or anywhere near him is not because of some useless, unnecessary soccer rivalry. It's not about a game. It's because Reed Jackson is a punk."

Con's jaw clenches and tics for a few seconds as if he can't even bear to talk about Reed. He can't even bear to say his name in front of me.

"He's a rich punk who only cares about himself. I know him and I know guys like him. Guys like him are selfish, untrustworthy, and reckless. Guys like him don't care about rules or people. They only care about themselves. Guys like him can't handle responsibilities. They leave without so much as a glance back at what they're leaving behind."

I don't know why, but it feels like Con is speaking from experience, but before I can ask him, he goes on, "So the reason we want you to stay away from him is because he's not good for you. He's not worthy of you. He doesn't deserve you. Do you understand what I'm saying to you, Callie? He's not the guy for you. You need to stay away from him because you deserve better and because you're smart. You're smarter than the rest of the girls who fall victim to him."

Chapter 5

I'm running from him.

Well, not exactly.

It's not as if he's chasing after me or anything. He's not.

In fact, if you look at him sauntering down the hallways, being worshipped by guys and girls alike, you'd think that Friday night never happened.

That I never went to his party. He never caught me while I was trying to duck out. And I never danced for him.

The only evidence of that night is that nasty split lip and the bruise on his jaw.

Even after four days, it looks just as angry and red as it must have when Ledger laid it on him.

Every time I see it, my heart twists in my chest.

My legs itch to go over to him and touch it. Touch him.

But I can't.

That's why I'm running.

The second I see him, I turn around and leave, which I usually did anyway, but these days I'm ruthless. If he comes in my line of vision, I duck my head. The second I start to think about him, I shut it the eff down.

Besides, it's not as if *he* is thinking about me.

As I said, looking at him, you wouldn't even know that Friday night happened.

Not to mention, there are girls taking care of his bruise. In fact, I saw a girl from junior year caressing it out in the courtyard today.

I think she even reached up and kissed it. I'm not sure. I didn't wait to see what she would do once she'd gone up on her tiptoes.

So yeah, I need to move on and consider Friday night an anomaly and focus on what's important.

The upcoming dance show in which I'm the lead.

Yes, I am.

I don't even know how it happened. Because I'm a freshman and they never pick a freshman. They usually go for a junior or senior.

I'm actually very proud.

If only this wasn't so hard.

I mean, it's a fairly easy routine. The dance itself is a mix of classical ballet and contemporary choreography. There's nothing here that I haven't done before.

But.

I cannot nail down the last part of it. I'm having trouble with holding the positions, with my calves being steady, with my toes bearing my weight.

So I'm basically having trouble with everything and I just want to give up and cry.

I mean, what kind of a ballerina am I if I can't get my toes to cooperate with me?

A sucky one.

School's been done for hours but I'm in the auditorium, trying to get it right.

I can't though.

Because I'm tired now. My limbs are exhausted and I want to go home and just soak in a bathtub for hours, clean up the scrapes on my toes, bandage my ankle and take a bucketful of painkillers.

So I pack up my things, unplug the stereo and bring it to the storage closet located backstage. Opening the door, I switch on the light and set the heavy equipment down on one of the shelves on the far end.

The moment I do though, I hear something, a creak and a footstep, a click, and I spin around already knowing — *hoping* — who it would be.

And I'm right.

It's him.

He's leaning against the now closed door of the storage closet, his gray eyes glued to me. And just at the sight of him, at the fact that my secret, dangerous wish has come true, I stop breathing.

I don't need to breathe anyway because euphoria is bursting in my veins like firecrackers.

He's here.

Here. Finally.

My heart races as if it's been waiting and waiting for him to come find me.

Even though I've been making every effort to stay away from him and to run.

Even though the words that come out of my mouth are the exact opposite of what I'm feeling. "Y-you can't be in here."

Good.

Good, this is smart.

This is what I should be saying to him.

He's a bad guy, remember?

It doesn't matter what I feel.

It doesn't even make sense that I feel these things.

In response, Reed shifts on his feet and settles even more against the door like he has no plans to go anywhere. "Yeah, why not?"

"Because Ledger is here," I tell him, my own feet doing what they've been doing for the past few days, itching to go to him as soon as I see him.

But I dig my toes into the ground and stop them.

"So?"

God.

Why is this so appealing? His reckless, daredevil, *rule-breaking* attitude.

Maybe because I've never broken a rule myself.

Maybe because I've never *seen* anyone break a rule with so little care where the repercussions are so dire, AKA getting beaten up by my brothers.

I bring my arms back and grab hold of the shelf behind me. Just so I'll stay put. Even though it's getting harder and harder to do that.

"He's at the library, waiting for me to finish up so he can take me home. And I can't be late. Not after…" I trail off, glancing at the bruise, still so fresh looking and red, sitting on the left side of his jaw.

His jaw that is shadowed with a light stubble that he must hate.

Under my gaze, he thumbs it. "Friday night."

He remembers…

Like a fool, I think of that first.

It doesn't matter whether he remembers or not.

What matters is, he needs to leave.

Nodding, I whisper, "Yes."

"So they're keeping an eye on you."

Not them.

As I said, my brothers have given me all the freedom. They've always trusted me.

This is me.

I'm trying to make up for last Friday.

After how they all came to apologize and bring me cupcakes, I'm doing this to make up for the lying.

It might be too much for some girls – teenagers lie, right? – and I get that.

But then those girls don't have awesome brothers like mine. They don't share a unique bond with their siblings like I do.

I shake my head. "It's me. I lied to them."

He hums thoughtfully. "And found yourself in the clutches of a villain."

My heart skips a beat when he says it, the term I called him that night.

And it's a perfect term too.

He does look like a villain. A gorgeous villain.

With beautiful wolf eyes and marble skin. A jaw so sharp and cheekbones so high. Broad shoulders and a massive chest that tapers into a slim waist.

Every part of his body looms large and threatening.

Even that bruise adds to his danger.

"You should go," I tell him, breathless.

"But here you are, aren't you? In my clutches again," he murmurs, completely ignoring my statement.

I am.

I have no escape either. I glance at the door behind him, which believe it or not is difficult because he's covering it all up with his towering body.

"Why's the door locked?" I ask him.

"You've been running from me," he says.

"I'm not," I lie, wondering how he even knows when he's been too busy with his awesome life.

"And I'm not letting you run from me again."

His words hang in the air menacingly and I ask, "*Letting* me?"

"Yeah."

I frown at him. "Isn't that… criminal?"

"Is it?"

I exhale sharply. "Yes, it is. You can't lock a girl in a closet against her will. Just because you don't want her to run."

Something like amusement passes over his features. "Right. I think I heard about something like that."

"You —"

"But also, I don't think I'm holding her against her will. Am I?"

I swallow and grab hold of the edge of the shelf tightly. "Why don't I scream and you can find out if it's against my will or not?"

It only makes him smirk. "Why don't you? Let's see if it reaches your brother and he comes to save you." He flexes his fist by his side. "I'd love to give him a matching bruise for last Friday."

My heart jumps. "You wouldn't."

"Wouldn't I?"

"No. Because… Because you apologized to him that night," I remind him, trying to tamp down shivers at the thought of him keeping that promise to me. "You kept your promise."

"And that means what?"

"It means that maybe you're not as bad as they say you are."

"Yeah, no. I'm exactly as bad as they say I am." He spreads his hands as if in a magnanimous gesture. "I'd be happy to show you if you like. All you have to do is scream."

I study him for a long, careful moment before saying,

"How did you even know that I was here?"

"I saw you dancing through the window," he says.

"You did?" I ask, surprised.

"Uh-huh." His eyes grow heated, and all my ire seems to be on the verge of melting. "You were spinning. So fast. And I stopped."

"Why?"

He licks his lips and I'm reminded of how excited he looked that night when I danced for him.

When he called me a fairy.

God.

God.

He called me that, didn't he?

I've been trying not to think about it. Not to think about his words, the words no one has ever said to me before.

Fairy.

"Because apparently when you spin, I stop. When you dance, I have to watch," he says in a low, slightly rough voice.

And suddenly I feel the same way. As I did that night.

All hot and restless. My limbs buzzing.

"I sucked," I say.

He frowns. "What?"

I'm not sure if I should tell him this. But I'm going to.

I don't know why but I have to tell him the truth.

So swallowing, I whisper, "My routine. I can't do it. I-I mean, I can. But I'm screwing it all up."

His frown only grows. "Someone tell you that?"

I shake my head. "No. Everyone has been super kind

so far. But I-I'm supposed to hold this pose, a developpé écarté devant, at the end for like eight counts before coming down on my knees, but I could only do it for like four or something. And even then, my calves were shaking, and do you even know how big of a crime that is? Not being able to hold straight and still. A very big crime. Huge."

It is.

And if they don't kick me out then I'll just quit myself because this is a disgrace.

For some reason, his lips twitch. "I don't think anyone would notice how long you stood on your toes."

I narrow my eyes at him, at his amusement. "Why not?"

"Because they'll be too distracted at the sight of you down on your knees." He tips his chin at me. "Especially in that."

All of a sudden it hits me that I'm in costume.

I've been wearing this for three hours now and I completely forgot. I completely forgot that this is the first time Reed is seeing me in this.

A white leotard and a light green tutu.

Not to mention, I also have wings.

They are heavy — although after wearing them for so long, my shoulders have gone numb so I don't feel their weight anymore — and made of white fur. They're slung over my shoulders with white ribbon-like strings and rustle across my spine and arms.

Like a fairy…

I've been wearing leotards and tutus all my life so until he looks at me from top to bottom, I don't realize how revealing it can be.

How tight the costume is and how it fits me like a second skin. How it highlights every lithe muscle, every delicate bone in my body.

How exposed I am.

Even more than I was back in the woods.

And before I can stop myself, I say, "It's my tutu."

When he lifts his eyes back to my face, they're the darkest that I've seen them.

Liquid and fiery.

"Yeah?" he rasps in an almost indulgent tone.

I bring my trembling hands forward and trace the frilly fabric. "It's like a skirt."

"And what are those?"

He points to my feet and I look down. "Uh, they're called pointe shoes." I chuckle as I look up. "You know, people say that ballerinas have the ugliest feet. They're all swollen and bruised and cut up and –"

"People are stupid."

"But –"

I stop talking because something makes him move.

I don't know what it is but he straightens up and I'm wondering what the chances are that he'll stay put where he is, by the door, when he starts walking toward me.

It's not a big space so by the time I gather my wits to ask him what the heck he's doing, he's already here.

He's already touching me.

Not me, per se.

He's touching my wings. Or one of them actually.

Standing over me like a threat or something, a delicious, gorgeous threat in a white hoodie and a pulsating bruise, Reed reaches out and brushes a finger along the edge of my wing. Crazily, my spine arches up at the touch. As if he's touching my skin instead of my fake wing.

His eyes drop to my bowed body and if he couldn't see the shape of it before, he can sure see it now.

He can see the bones of my ribs, the hollow of my stomach. My really small but jutting out breasts.

"What are these wings for?" he asks, bringing his eyes up to mine.

"F-for my character."

"What character is that?"

"I'm a fairy."

Somehow his eyes grow all heated even as a slight lopsided smile pulls up his lips. "So I was right, huh?"

"I –"

He rubs the fur between his fingers as he continues, "You *are* a fairy. You dance like a fairy." His eyes flick over my face, my bun. "You look like one too."

I lose my breath for a second.

I also lose my heartbeats. My rational thoughts.

That's the only explanation for why my legs stretch up and I get closer to him. "I'm a stupid fairy though."

"How so?"

"Because I fall in love with my enemy. In the song."

"Your enemy."

"Yes, a human. He's supposed to hunt fairies."

"And what about him?" he asks, his fingers still playing with my wing and his eyes going back and forth between mine. "Does he fall in love with you too?"

"Yes." I swallow, my own fingers fisting my tutu. "Or I think he does. But he's lying."

"Why?"

"Because he's using me. He wants to trap me and bring me back to his family. I'm supposed to be his first hunt."

"What a fucking asshole."

"Everyone warns me about him. All my fairy friends and my family. But I don't listen to them. I think he's a hero."

"But he's not, is he?"

"No, he's the villain in my story."

A fire rages in his eyes, hot and so vivid that it burns me. "Yeah, I know something about villains."

My heart twists in my chest for some reason. "His name is Romeo."

"Romeo."

"Yeah. In the song."

"And you must be Juliet then."

I nod. "I'm actually Juliet." Then, "My name. Calliope Juliet Thorne."

"Calliope Juliet Thorne," he repeats in his rich deep voice. Also smooth.

And it feels as if instead of plucking at the edges of my wing, he's swirling the ends of my nerves with his long fingers. And he's doing it somewhere in the small of my back so that my spine bows for him even more.

He appreciates my efforts too.

He runs his eyes over my stretched-out body once more.

"And you're Reed Roman Jackson."

"You know my name, huh?"

"It's not a secret. Your full name. Girls chant it pretty often. Like a prayer."

He smirks. "Do they?"

"Yes," I answer, slightly irked. "They also call you Romeo."

His eyes narrow. "What?"

I nod. "Because everyone knows that Roman is just another version of Romeo."

"Yeah, bullshit."

It's my turn to smirk at his irritation. "It's okay. They do it with love. But you should be careful."

"Of what?"

"Of coming anywhere near me." I raise my eyebrows. "I'm Juliet, remember? Our names are tragic. Shakespearean. We're bad luck together. So maybe you shouldn't lock me up in a closet and should stay away from me instead."

"Or what?"

I eye his bruise then. "Or you get beaten up by my brothers."

"I told you I can handle myself."

"You know –"

"Besides what does Shakespeare know anyway?"

"What, Shakespeare knows everything."

"Does he?"

"Yes."

He cocks his head to the side as he says, "Well, how about we do something about that then?"

"Do something about what?"

"Our names."

"What?"

Instead of giving me an explanation, Reed moves his eyes away from my face and focuses on my wings. My white fur wings that are suddenly growing too heavy and too light all at the same time.

"How about I call you by my name and you call me by yours?" he asks huskily.

"Your name."

"Fairy," he murmurs, his eyes coming back to my face and burning me alive yet again. "I get to call you Fairy."

I swallow.

Fairy.

He wants to call me Fairy.

I don't... I don't know what to say.

So I just repeat his words. "You want to call me Fairy."

Instead of answering me though, he roves his wolf eyes over my face once more before stepping back and taking his touch away.

"See you around, Fae."

With that he begins to leave.

As if he didn't just obliterate my breaths, my balance with that one word.

Fae.

A second later though, he stops and fishes something out of his pocket. Keeping his eyes on me, at my heaving, shuddering body, he puts it on the shelf by his side.

"Almost forgot about it," he says. "It's for you."

It's hard to drag my eyes away from his penetrating ones but I want to know what he brought me. It's an envelope, purple and pretty, and looking out of place in this dark closet.

"What is it?" I ask, glancing back at him.

"An invitation."

"To what?"

"A party."

"You're inviting me to a party?"

"No." He explains, "My sister is. It's Pest's birthday this weekend. She wanted me to give it to you. I'm just the messenger."

Finally he leaves, and this time he doesn't stop or turn back.

Tempest.

His sister.

The girl I met at the game last week and who dragged me to his party.

I've been thinking about her, wondering if I'd get to see her again. I really liked her.

And now as her brother is unlocking the door and leaving, I'm thinking about the fact that he calls her Pest. And how he came here to do her bidding, to give me the invitation, which I'm pretty sure she must've bugged him about until he relented.

And *God* I have to go to him right now.

Snatching the envelope and clutching it in my hands, I run after him.

He's almost at the edge of the stage and I call out, "Roman."

He stops then.

Slowly, he turns around and looks at me.

I know that I should let him go. I know that I shouldn't have stopped him.

I know that doing this is foolish. And maybe I am that. Foolish.

But I don't care.

Staring into his piercing eyes, I hug the envelope to my chest and say, "If you call me Fae, then I get to call you Roman."

Chapter 6

Tempest and I are awesome friends now.

Best friends even.

It didn't take us long to become that. In fact, I think we became good friends as soon as we met at the game. But our friendship was sealed at her birthday party.

Which I made sure to attend and which wasn't an easy thing to do.

I knew it wouldn't be.

I knew my brothers would freak out. Already me going to that one party has created so much drama and now I wanted to go to another one.

But I was going and I wasn't going to lie about it.

So I told them and, well, it didn't go well.

Definitely not with Ledger, who kept grumbling about it for that whole week, pacing and stomping and cursing.

We had four family meetings about it. *Four.*

So family meetings are a tradition in our house.

Conrad established it long ago, so whenever there's something that might be important– from where to go on vacation over the summer or Ledger getting a new truck to switching from whole wheat pasta to spinach pasta – we all get a say.

I think it's his way of keeping all of us in the loop and functioning as a family.

So that whole week, leading up to the party, there were long discussions over dinner where Ledger would just curse and say no to everything. Stellan, who would join us over the phone, would try to reason with him and tell him that I'm not a child and at least I didn't lie like the last time.

While Shep, again over the phone, would make stupid jokes all the while siding with Ledger.

Until Conrad put a stop to it all and declared that Ledger would go with me.

"It's not that I don't trust you. I don't trust where you're going. So if you want to go, Ledge will go with you."

That seemed to satisfy all my brothers and so that was how I went to Tempest's birthday party, with Ledger – and some of his friends, who he invited along without even telling me – as my bodyguards.

Which was fine.

I mean, it was an overkill but I understood where Ledger was coming from. The party was going to be full of people from the Mustang camp and he wanted some of his own friends there.

I was just glad to go and to hang out with Tempest, who was glad to see me as well.

Together, we made every effort to forget the fact that our brothers and their respective friends were glaring at each other from across the room. Or that tensions were running high.

At some point during the night, our brothers made a pact: sisters are off-limits.

Meaning they would continue to fight and be at odds with each other but none of them were allowed to bring their sisters into it. So Reed can't use me to provoke my brother, and Ledger can't use Tempest to provoke Reed.

As weird as this pact was, it came as a relief.

Because I do think that Tempest is into my idiot brother and I don't want her being used in the name of their stupid rivalry.

If a pact keeps her safe, then I'm all for it.

Besides, I do want to be her friend.

And ever since her birthday party, Tempest has been coming down from New York every weekend to hang out with me at my house and she always looks for ways to talk to Ledger.

Who always looks for ways to avoid her because she's a Jackson.

And he hates all Jacksons.

Especially the one by the name of Reed Roman Jackson.

Or just Roman.

Not that I've gotten a chance to call him that after the first time.

Because while Tempest is trying everything to tempt Ledger, her brother is trying everything to stick to the pact.

Yup.

Who would've thought that Reed would be so good at keeping promises?

At school, he goes about his normal business.

And by business, I mean he always has girls around him. He's always surrounded by his friends who also happen to be the loudest of all, attracting all kinds of attention. At practice and at games, he provokes my brother and my brother retaliates and vice versa. They stay on opposite sides of hallways and the cafeteria like they always have.

Most of all, he ignores me like he's always done.

He passes by me in the hallway without sparing me a glance. If we happen to find ourselves in the same place at the same time, he hardly knows that I'm there. In fact, when I go to his house to see Tempest like she comes to mine to visit me, he's never there.

I know it shouldn't bother me, but it does.

That's the only reason why I'm letting Tempest do this.

She's got it in her head that I'm perfect for her brother.

I've told her a million times that I'm not. Her brother isn't even interested in girlfriends. Not to mention, my brothers – Ledger specifically – would kill him if I ever got involved with him. But she hasn't listened so far and up until now, I've shot down all her ideas to get me closer to Reed.

Until today.

I mean, this isn't a plan to get close to her brother per se. Her brother isn't even home; I'm at Tempest's this Saturday afternoon.

It's a plan to give me more confidence in my own skin. To

make me think that I can be sexy too.

Like all his girlfriends, or girls.

Who somehow are masters at smoky eyes and sultry make-up. Also all of them have dark, sexy hair, unlike my stupid blonde good-girl tresses.

No, don't think about that, Callie. This is about female em-powerment. This is about you, not him!

Anyway, I'm wearing one of Tempest's dresses. A black mini-dress that also happens to be strapless, which hits me mid-thigh, along with her heels. On top of all this, she's done my make-up and curled my blonde hair.

All in all, I do think that I look sexy.

After Tempest dresses me up like a doll, we venture out to go to the mall like this. I was happy to stay home and lounge around all dressed up but she says that if I want confidence, then I need to go out and get it myself.

And I do get it.

Because guys have been leering at me, at us, ever since we stepped out of the house. And it is great at first but as time passes, I start to get tired.

My feet start to kill me and after pulling down my dress a million times, I don't think I like this all that much.

All this unwanted attention and guys staring at my butt so openly.

I tell Tempest that I want to go home and relax and so she calls for her driver to come pick us up.

It's a good thing because I don't think I can walk in these shoes anymore.

Only my happiness is short-lived because instead of a driver, her brother shows up in a white flash, his Mustang.

He takes one look at the both of us and his wolf eyes grow furious as he growls, "Get in."

Which we do.

Tempest and I are in the back seat while Reed drives in a seething silence. When I catch Tempest's eye in the darkened interior of the car, she winks at me happily and that's how I know.

That's how I know that she never called the driver. She called *him*.

That *scheming*... non-friend.

Because we're not friends anymore. She lied to me.

Not only that, as soon as we reach their big, sprawling house, she jumps out of the car with a happy goodbye thrown at me.

Although her brother doesn't let her go so easily.

"Straight to your room," he growls again, the only words he's spoken after his commanding *get in*. "Now. And put some fucking clothes on, we're going to have a talk."

Her shoulders droop and she mumbles something before turning to me, winking and running away, leaving me alone with him.

Oh my God.

Oh my *God*, I'm gonna kill her. I'm so gonna kill her right now.

Actually, I'm so gonna kill *him*.

For being so... authoritative and angry.

Only he also makes me want to rub my legs together

in restlessness when he talks like that, in his deep commanding voice.

But whatever.

I throw open the door and jump out, totally charged up to go after Tempest and make her pay for this. But I don't get too far. In fact, I don't even get to take more than a few steps away from his Mustang because there's something stopping me.

Or someone.

How he made it out of the car and over to my side so fast, I don't know. All I know is that I can't go anywhere as long as he stands before me.

Or rather, as long as he's backing me up into his car.

As soon as my spine hits the cold metal, I shiver and words jar out of me. "Let me go."

He doesn't.

Frankly, I didn't expect him to.

But then I also didn't expect him to lean forward. I didn't expect him to put his arm on the roof of his car, just by my side, effectively stopping me from leaving.

Although I should have. Expected it, I mean.

If he can lock me up in a closet so I don't get to run from him, he can do anything.

"What are you doing?" I ask.

In response, he runs his eyes all over my body, slowly, methodically, as if making a point before raising them back to my face. "Looking at you."

Again, I get the urge to rub my thighs together at his low, heated tone. "Why?"

"Because that's what you want, don't you? You want me to look at you."

"I do not," I lie.

When did I become such a liar?

I thought I was the good girl.

He knows I'm lying too because a smirk breaks out on his ruby-red, crescent-shaped mouth. Only it has a dangerous edge, a humorless quality. "Yeah, you do. Why else would you be wearing something like that? Something that..." He looks me up and down again, a cursory and yet lingering glance. "Leaves very little to my imagination."

My imagination.

As if.

I put my sweaty palms on his Mustang so my balance doesn't falter. "That's extremely arrogant of you, don't you think? To assume that. That I'd wear something just to get your attention."

Never mind that I did. I mean, subconsciously.

Okay maybe a *little* consciously but whatever.

He dips his chin in a condescending manner. "It's the truth though, isn't it?"

In response, I raise mine, just to look defiant. "No, it's not. And this is a perfectly normal dress."

"Is it?"

"Yes."

I'm not sure what's happening tonight but everything that I'm saying is making him angrier and angrier.

And none of that is even remotely bothersome to me.

Not even when he leans further down, shaking the car at my back and bringing his wolf eyes, which I cannot look away from, even closer.

"Because I don't think that a *perfectly normal dress* would highlight every fucking curve of your tight ballerina body," he says with clenched teeth. "Would it? Or that when you walk in it, your perky tits would be dangerously close to jiggling out. And the whole world could see the cheeks of your juicy, tight ass."

For a number of seconds after he's finished talking, I'm unable to believe the things he's said.

For a number of seconds, I simply blink up at him.

I've never ever heard anyone talk about my body in such graphic, derogatory terms. Because it is all derogatory, isn't it?

I should slap him in the face. I should.

I shouldn't feel a rush in my chest that beads my nipples to achy points or shift on my feet just to rub my butt against his Mustang.

And the fact that he can make me feel and do all these inappropriate, less than respectable, *bad* things makes me say, "You're an asshole."

At my curse – which was so effortless for me, dangerously effortless when it comes to him – he flinches slightly before growing even more furious.

"I am. And in case your four older, overprotective brothers forgot to mention it to you, assholes like me don't play by the rules. Assholes like me take whatever they want, whenever they want. And I'm probably the worst of them all."

My breaths have gone haywire so my next words come

out thin and breathless. "What does that mean?"

"It *means*…" He pauses to bring his other arm up as well, putting it on the roof of his Mustang and making a cage around me. "That I'm the kind of asshole that keeps your brothers up at night. I'm the reason girls like you have a curfew. I'm the reason your mommy sits you down in your room and warns you about boys. She tells you how rotten they can be, how corrupt. How they'll lie and cheat and do anything to stick their hands under your dress. I'm the reason your daddy locks your door at night. And he puts you in a bedroom on the top floor so no one can climb in. He bars your windows. He stands guard outside of your door on the off chance that I somehow still find a way in. And I fucking do. You know how?"

"H-how?"

He shakes the car again, making me teeter on my heels, unbalancing my world. "Because I'm the kind of asshole who'd break down any door. I'd climb a thousand stories. I'd climb a fucking tower. Just to be able to get into your room at night. Just to be able to see you. And I bet you wear those lacy white nighties, don't you?"

"Yes, sometimes."

"Yeah, I'd pull apart all the bars in your window. I'd fucking go to war with all four of your brothers just to be able to see you in one of those. Just to be able to get a peek of your creamy, dancer legs in something like that. Just to see if I can catch a glimpse of something else too, in your thin white nightie." He leans in another inch as he continues, "You don't want me to do that, do you? You don't want me to force my way into your room at night, while your brothers are sleeping down the hall somewhere just so I could look at you, at your tight little body, in your white nightie."

I do.

I so do.

I want him to force his way inside my room just so he can look at me.

And as soon as this thought flashes through my mind, I shake my head. "No."

"Yeah. Because let's face it, I get a peek of you in that thing and I won't be able to stop myself from taking it too far."

"Too far."

His eyes are glowing now. "Yeah, I get a peek of you in your nightie, I'll be doing everything that I can to fucking touch it. To somehow push the hem up your thighs or pull the straps down your shoulders, just so I can get my hands on your naked body. But again, you don't want me to do that, do you, Fae?"

Oh God.

How is it that I feel both relieved and restless that he called me that? How is it that I've been waiting and waiting for him to call me by his name one more time?

It's a wonder that I can still shake my head and say what he wants me to say when all I want to say is yes. Yes, yes, yes.

"No," I whisper and arch my body, up and toward him as if offering him to touch it.

"Yeah, that's what I thought. And why not?" he asks, the strings of his hoodie oscillating in front of me in a hypnotic rhythm. "Tell me why you don't want me to touch you, to grope your fucking body like the villain that I am."

I can't remember.

I can't remember anything right now.

But I guess all of this is so ingrained in my brain that I don't even have to think about it, about the rivalry and soccer and hatred. My lips move on their own. "Because of my b-brothers."

Satisfaction bursts over his features even as his jaw tightens for a second. "You wouldn't want to betray them now, would you?"

"No."

How many times have I said no now, I wonder?

And how many times have I wanted to say yes?

I'm a fool.

A fool, a fool, a fool.

But he makes it so easy. He makes it so easy to be stupid and reckless and thoughtless.

He makes it so easy to be foolish.

"Good." He approves with a short nod. "So you're going to be careful now, aren't you? You're going to wear your daisy fresh dresses and your ballet flats. You're going to braid your hair like a good girl and you're going to stop begging for my attention. You're going to *stop* making me look at you."

His words, almost snarled from his mouth and dripping in condescension, penetrate my drugged-up mind and make me frown. They make me stand a little taller in my stupid heels when he moves away from me.

And I tell him with as much authority as I can muster right now, "Then you have to stop watching me."

Reed was in the process of taking another step back and dismissing me. But my words stop him. They make him frown. "What?"

Good.

I'm glad.

If he can give me ultimatums, then I can issue them too.

I raise my trembling chin and say, "You have to stop coming to my practice every day."

Because that's what he does.

He comes to my after-hours practice and he watches me dance.

Every day after school, when I practice in the auditorium because I still haven't nailed down my routine, he comes in.

He sits in the third row, not too far away from the stage and not too close. I don't know why. And he watches me spin and turn and leap around the stage with my wings on my back.

He watches me like he did the first night at the party.

All eager and intense and at the edge of his seat.

And I dance for him in the same way as well. All restless and excited.

After the pact I was afraid that he'd stop. I was afraid that he wouldn't watch me dance anymore. But he didn't and thank God for that.

Because somehow, I've gotten addicted to dancing for him.

Somehow, I've become addicted to the way he looks at me. Addicted to the way his shoulders seem to loosen up the longer I dance. How he sits back and sprawls out on the seat as if this is the best part of his day, me dancing for him.

So sometimes I dance for him just because he wants me to.

I abandon my practice, pick a song that I love and spin for him like the ballerina I am.

His ballerina.

But it's stupid, isn't it? And dangerous.

He's right.

He's the worst asshole of all, the biggest villain that my brothers have warned me about.

And I can't betray my brothers – Ledger – no matter what my heart keeps telling me.

So this is the best course of action, staying away like we always have.

"And why's that?" he challenges.

I press my hands harder on the Mustang. "Because you're right. This is stupid. I never should've worn this *stupid* dress."

Yeah, everything happened because of this stupid freaking dress.

If I wasn't wearing this, then I'd be safely tucked away inside Tempest's room, watching something silly on her laptop instead of standing out here in these torturous heels under his *torturous* scrutiny.

"Why did you then?"

"Because I wanted to see what it felt like..." I trail off when I realize what I was going to say.

Of course, he hones in on that and his features grow alert. "Felt like what?"

Well, I was stupid enough to bring it up, wasn't I?

I can be stupid, stupid, *stupid* enough to finish it too.

What do I have to lose anyway?

I fist the dress and stand tall in my heels. "I wanted to see what it felt like to be sexy. To be tempting for a day. To feel like all the girls at school. All the girls you hang out with."

There. I said it.

It's over. My humiliation is complete.

Can I just go home now and never ever come back here, to his house?

"You wanted to feel like the girls I hang out with."

Oh, so it's not complete yet. My humiliation.

Fine.

Whatever. I can deal with this.

"Yes." I sigh. "I wanted to feel sexy and confident and, I don't know, just not like a good girl all the time. But I *am* a good girl, aren't I? Because I hate this dress. And I hate these heels and I hate you too. So from now on, I'm not going to dance for you and you can't come watch me like it's your right or something. I'm not for your personal entertainment, okay?"

Then I throw my hands in the air and snap, "In fact from now on, you should ask one of your girlfriends to dance for you. I'm sure they'd be happy to accommodate your every whim like they always are. So, is there anything else you need to say to me, because I'd like to leave now."

He stares at me and stares at me with an inscrutable expression until I start to feel like a freak show for going off like that.

But he deserved it, didn't he?

He…

"They're not my girlfriends," he murmurs after a bit.

Something about his casual answer irritates me even further and I snap, "Yeah, do they know that?"

"They do, yes." He shrugs then but there's this wild, wild intensity on his face, in his body too, looking all tight and strung up. "With me, they always know. I don't do girlfriends."

"And why? Why are you so special that you don't do girlfriends?"

"Because I don't. It's not my style. I don't believe in love and shit."

Of course.

A typical guy. I have four brothers and two of whom are complete players like him; I know.

They're the same.

Wild and untamable.

And I don't know why he's watching me like he's performing some kind of experiment. "Well then, as I said, you should ask your other girls to dance for you and leave me alone."

His scrutiny isn't over yet.

Not for another five or six seconds, and then, "You sound like you're jealous, Fae."

I gasp. Almost.

How dare he?

How freaking dare he?

I shift on my stupid heels again.

"You'd know, wouldn't you?" I raise my eyebrows. "Be-

cause you sounded like you were jealous when you thought that
the world was looking at my juicy, tight ass, *Roman*."

It's his turn to blink.

Not that it makes him look intimidated by me or something like that.

In fact, I'm the one who loses all the air in her lungs because I've been dying, *dying*, to call him that. And to say it like
that, blurting it out, makes me stumble on my heels.

He's just taken aback, I think.

Not by what I said, but what he says next, almost to himself, as if he's surprised by it. "I was."

"You were?"

He looks into my wide, shocked eyes. "Yeah. And I don't
like that."

"Being jealous?"

"Yes."

His frown is so… adorable. It's such a tame word for a
guy like him who's made of all sharp and dangerous edges.

But that's what I feel right now.

That he's so vulnerable and adorable in this moment with
his honesty and so I have to be honest too. "M-me neither."

He opens and closes his fists as if he can't decide what he
wants to do with his fingers. He can't decide what he wants to
do in a situation like this and I can't wait to see what he *does* do.

Then with a sharp breath that pushes out his massive
chest, he becomes himself.

He becomes dark in his intentions and dangerous in his
beauty.

He looks me up and down in his villainous way before taking a couple of steps closer to me and I go a couple of steps back.

"So how about I make you another promise?" he offers like the devil he is.

"What promise?" I ask, looking up at him.

But not for long because right in front of my eyes, he does something incredible.

He does something that I never even imagined he would do.

Right in front of my eyes, Reed Roman Jackson slowly comes down on his knees.

The sight of it is so shocking that my hand sticks out on its own and grabs hold of his shoulder. His hoodie.

"I don't know... what you're doing," I whisper, looking into his eyes, which are on level with mine.

Because he's so, so tall.

His answer is to smile lopsidedly and grab my ankle.

Before I can even utter a word, he's taken off my shoe and given me my breaths back. When he goes for the other one and brings me back down to earth, taking off the added four inches of my height, I want to hug him.

I don't even care that now he reaches the top of my head easily.

I don't even care that the stark difference in our sizes makes me look all helpless in front of him.

"Tell me about your promise," I whisper, putting my other hand on his shoulder as well and clutching his soft hoodie.

His gaze turns liquid. "You take off that dress and braid your hair."

"And?"

His fingers still circle my ankle, squeezing. "And you dance only for me."

"What would I get in return?"

"And in return, I won't ask any other girls to dance for me." Another squeeze of my ankle and I bite my lip. "Only you."

Only me.

He just said that.

And maybe it's not exactly what a girl hopes to hear from a guy. It's not a declaration or anything. Just a little promise. And for now, it seems like enough. It seems enough to make me smile and wiggle my free toes on the ground in happiness.

It seems enough that I step closer to him and my bare feet graze his bent knees. "On one condition."

"What?"

I dare to touch the ends of his dark hair; they're as soft and silky as his hoodie. "I hear you love your Mustang."

His eyes narrow in suspicion. "I do."

I want to touch his stubble as well, the thing that appears every evening to bother him, but I'm not that bold so I satisfy myself with playing with his soft, soft hair.

"People say that she's your baby."

His hands go to my waist. "She is."

I suck in a breath at how easily he can span my slender torso. "I want you to give me a ride."

He digs his thumbs in the soft flesh of my stomach. "Ride

to where?"

I don't even have to think about the answer, and good thing too, because all my thoughts are gone except the one.

He's touching me so possessively, like how a sculptor touches their creation maybe, with authority, with a sense of ownership. "Back to those woods where the party was that night."

He studies my face for a few seconds. "You want me to take you back to the woods."

"Yes."

"Alone? At night."

I nod, biting my lip.

"What do you think your four older, overprotective brothers would say about that? About me breaking the pact."

Oh right.

The stupid pact.

"I won't say anything to them. Ever," I promise, so easily falling into his trap.

"You won't."

"No. And my curfew isn't until eleven."

That brings a smirk on his face and makes him grip me tighter, like he's never letting me get away now. "Curfew."

I grip him tighter too because I'm not running away either.

I don't know when it happened, but I've become reckless now.

A girl who wears provocative dresses for a villain and asks him to take her out to the woods at night.

"Uh-huh." I nod. "You can bring me back here before

that and no one will ever know."

"Are you asking me to keep another secret, Fae?" he rasps, looking all wild and wicked. "Because you know my price, don't you?"

"Yes. And I'll give it to you."

"You will, huh."

"Yeah, I'll dance for you. For as long as you want."

Because I'm his Fae, the dancing fairy and he's my Roman, the wild mustang.

Chapter 7

I imagine telling my brothers about him.

About Roman.

I daydream about all the things I'll tell them. I'll start with how amazing he is with Tempest. This is something my brothers will definitely relate to, him being an older, overprotective brother like them.

I'll tell them that last month when Tempest got really sick and she made one call to Reed, he abandoned his classes and his practice for the day and drove up to New York City. He argued with the teachers, with the headmaster even, and got her out of the dorm within the hour. He brought her back home and for days, he took care of her.

I saw that myself.

That week, every day after school, I went to visit her and he'd be there, reminding her about meds, feeding her soup, *hovering* with a big frown and a grumpy face when she'd disobey.

I'll tell my brothers that it reminds me of how they take care of me when I get sick.

Then I'll tell them that like them, he buys me Peanut Butter Blossoms.

One day we were driving by Buttery Blossoms — he gives me a ride in his Mustang almost every time I go to their house to visit Tempest on weekends; at first, I thought she'd be mad at me for ditching her but she encourages it, me spending time with her brother — and I pointed it out through the window and told him all about it.

"So the special thing about them is that the crumb is peanut butter and the frosting is chocolate. When usually people have a *chocolate* crumb and *peanut butter* frosting. See? Special, right? But I can't eat too many. Ballet and all that. And the other day my partner told me that I was getting too heavy for him to lift. Can you believe that?" I chewed on my lips. "Maybe I should go on my juice fast this weekend. I can easily —"

I stopped talking when the car suddenly came to a halt and in a flash, he climbed out of it. I climbed out after him and watched him stride over to Buttery Blossoms.

A minute later, he came out holding a familiar pink box.

"Your partner is a pussy," he growled, thrusting it into my hands. "And juice fasts are fucking stupid."

And like an idiot, I hugged that box to my chest, blinked up at him and whispered, "You know, you shouldn't really curse this much, Roman."

His jaw clenched at that and his eyes grew all hot for a second before ordering, "Just get in the car."

And I did.

Yeah, I'll tell them about that.

All my brothers would love it because they think my juice fasts are stupid too.

And maybe if I tell them all this, they won't hate him so much.

Maybe Ledger won't fight with him.

Like he does one day at practice.

I'm not sure what happened because I wasn't there but when Reed shows up at the auditorium with a nasty split lip, I know.

That something happened between the two of them.

But the worst part is that he won't take care of it.

He absolutely *refuses* to take care of it in the coming days. Every time I ask him to, he goes, *it's fine.*

So one day I decide to take matters into my own hands and after *my* practice, as he's helping me pack up, I lock the door of the storage closet like he did that first time.

It's a bad idea, I think.

Because when he turns at the sound, glances at the door before glancing at me, the space shrinks and grows darker.

"Did you just lock the door?" he asks, his wolf eyes alert and pretty.

"Yes."

He leans against the shelf, folding his arms across his chest. "What about your brother who's waiting for you in the library?"

His hoodie's off and so I try not to look at the tiny hills

that his biceps make under his light-colored t-shirt. "Well, he can wait another ten minutes. I don't care."

A smirk appears on his lips, all split and still pretty. "Ten minutes, huh. Living on the edge, are we?"

I stand on the stepstool to get my hands on the first aid kit on the storage shelf by the door. "Yeah. He'll be fine."

"I don't think ten minutes is enough."

When I get it, I step down and turn to him. "Oh, it's enough. Trust me."

He hums, almost thoughtfully, still looking at my face. "I mean, sure. I could take care of you in ten minutes."

"Take care of me?"

Licking his lips, he nods. "Yeah. *Twice.*"

"Twice what?"

"Fair warning though," he goes on, ignoring my confusion. "I'll want to do it one more time just because I think I'll be fucking addicted to your taste. I'm already fucking addicted to your scent. Jasmine, is it? But you'll be trembling, and you'll tell me to stop so I'll decide to have mercy on you. Just this once."

Taste.

What...

My eyes go wide when I understand, when I get what he means.

And when I *do* get it, his features grow sharp, dangerous... seductive. "But then it'll be my turn, Fae. And trust me when I say that ten minutes is not going to cut it."

"It's n-not?"

He shakes his head slowly. "I'm not so easy to take care

of. When you're done taking care of me, you'll be going home with scraped up knees and swollen, dripping lips. Your brother will take one look at you and call the cops on me for doing bad things to his sister's pretty mouth in a storage closet. Not that I mind. But yeah, your math is slightly off there. I don't think ten minutes is enough."

The first aid kit's digging into my ribs by the time he finishes.

And I think I already have bruised knees and a swollen mouth, just because of the picture he's painted with his dirty words. I think my brother would know it anyway, that I was with him in a storage closet.

"It's geranium. And sugar. M-my scent."

"Geranium."

I nodded. "Yes, it's rare. It says on the bottle. I like rare body oils."

"I bet."

I hug the first aid kit to my chest even more tightly. "I…"

I don't know what to say except, *I'll do it.*

Oh my God, that's what I want to say, isn't it?

I want to tell him that I'll take care of him for as long as he wants.

I'm a ballerina. I'm not afraid of a little pain in my knees and bleeding skin.

I'll take care of him just like I dance for him in the woods when he puts on the music in his Mustang and sits on the hood to watch me.

Like he's the king of the world and I'm his slave girl.

Like he's my villain and I'm his ballerina.

But then he moves away from the shelf and approaches me, taking away all my thoughts.

He glances down at the first aid kit and my blinking, blushing face. "Do it."

My heart stops beating. "What?"

"You want to take care of my split lip, don't you?"

"Yes."

"Do it then."

Then without me having to say it, he drags the stepstool over with his foot for me to stand on. So it'll be easier for me to reach his injury. And all the while I take care of his bruise, my knees feel sore and my mouth feels swollen.

But I guess most of all, I want to tell my brothers how he helps me with my routine.

They all know my love for ballet and my ambition to go to Juilliard once I graduate from high school. It's my dream to dance for the New York City Ballet Company one day and all four of them have always been supportive of it.

So I know they'll definitely approve of the fact that Reed helps me practice.

Sure, it takes a little convincing on my part to get him to agree because when I first proposed the idea, his exact words were, "I'm not fucking twirling."

"Hey! That's extremely offensive," I told him from the stage. "Ballet isn't just twirling. There's like a hundred different things, *techniques*, that you do –"

"Well, you can call it whatever the fuck you want. I'm

still not fucking twirling."

I stood there, staring down at him in his seat in his favorite third row, all sprawled-out thighs and large chest, masculine and stubborn.

And gorgeous.

In that moment, I hated how gorgeous he was.

"I can't believe that you won't help me. I can't." I threw my hands up in the air. "And for what? Because ballet threatens your masculinity? That's it, isn't it? You think twirling will make you less of a guy. You think twirling is feminine. Meanwhile, you don't even care that chivalry is dying. That you've killed it. You've killed chivalry, Roman. Today. Right here, in this auditorium. And this is a crime scene. *Crime.* Scene. *Murder.* So –"

I went quiet when he stood up and started to walk toward me.

Before I knew it, he'd crossed all the rows and, putting his palms on the edge of the low-rising stage, lifted and swung himself onto the stage in one smooth motion. Just like that.

Without breaking a sweat or even taking a breath, he approached me and I asked, "What are you doing?"

"Showing you how chivalrous I can be."

"What?"

"Usually I don't mind being the bad guy, but I don't like to be accused of crimes I haven't committed. So if you want me to twirl, I'll fucking twirl and save you from distress and be your knight in fucking armor."

"Knight in shining armor," I said as soon as he finished.

He narrowed his eyes at me dangerously. "What?"

"You said knight in fucking armor. But it's knight in shining armor." I peered up at him through my eyelashes. "So you're my knight in *shining* armor."

"And if you want to be rescued, Fae, you need to start talking really soon and tell me what the fuck you want me to do before I change my mind."

And since then, he has helped me with my routine.

He has lifted me, assisted me with jumps and leaps.

He's made me better.

Surely if I tell them all of this, they won't hate him, will they?

They can't.

I mean, yes there's this rivalry and years of hatred between him and Ledger, years of them sabotaging each other on the field and at practice just to have the top spot.

But can't they move past it?

Can't Conrad see that Reed isn't as selfish as he thinks he is?

He's so much more than just a villain.

He's an amazing big brother. A protector.

A guy who keeps his promises. First by apologizing to Ledger that night, and then, by not even looking at another girl.

Because he hasn't.

Not since he made that promise to me, the night he took me for a ride in his Mustang for the first time.

I haven't seen him with a girl in the hallways. I haven't seen him flirting or taking any interest in them. In fact, the other day I overheard a few girls talking in the restroom during lunch.

About how Reed has seemed distant and distracted over the past few weeks.

See?

He can be a good guy, if he wants to be.

Only he doesn't want to be.

Not right now at least.

Not as I watch him on the soccer field, practicing with the team.

Well, there's no practice going on right now because the two star players are currently facing off against each other.

It's the same scene from that game weeks ago, the one that started everything.

Ledger is all angry and bunched up and Reed is cool and relaxed.

I know I should move on and not get involved. I never have before.

I was actually on my way to my own practice at the auditorium.

Tomorrow is my show that I've been practicing for for months and we're doing a full dress rehearsal.

Actually, tomorrow's also the day of the championship soccer game for Bardstown High and I'm still trying to figure out how I can both watch the game and make it to my own show.

But anyway, right now my plan was to just watch him play for a few minutes, hidden away behind the bleachers, and then leave to get to my own rehearsal.

But now I'm walking toward them, toward the crowd, the two camps, the Mustang and the Thorn.

Conrad and his assistant coaches are trying to settle everyone down. But when Con glares at Reed, snaps something at him and points to the bench, I know that it's only going to exacerbate the problem.

Reed glares back at Con and I grimace, thinking that he's going to say something to my brother and his coach, something disrespectful. But thankfully all he does is spit on the ground and wipe his mouth with the back of his hand and leave.

Or is about to, when something happens and it's Ledger.

Just as Reed is about to turn away, Ledger taunts, "Hey, Jackson! Can't wait to beat you tomorrow. Once and for all. You're going to regret not taking your dad's advice and quitting the team. You pollute everything you touch anyway."

Oh crap. Ledger!

He was leaving, *leaving* and my brother had to go and ruin it.

Reed's dad is a touchy subject.

I know that.

So apparently, his dad, the famous builder who owns everything in this town, hates the fact that Reed plays soccer. According to him, it's a huge waste of Reed's time because he wants his son to take over the business.

"My dad is an asshole," Tempest told me one day. "Like, a complete asshole. A negligent father. Bad, cheater of a husband. I'm glad I live far away from him. Though I miss my brother. I hate that he has to deal with our dad alone. And mom's no help. She lives in her own la-la land. But honestly though, Reed wouldn't let me deal with him anyway. He likes to protect me from stuff."

So I know there's tension between Reed and his dad.

I don't know the extent of it because Tempest was right, Reed *doesn't* like to talk about it, and I've tried to get him to only for him to shut down and grow angry.

Even right now, after Ledger's unnecessary taunt, he's done the same.

He's turned angry and rigid. Like stone.

Which only lasts for maybe two to three seconds before he fists his hands at his sides.

And then I already know what's going to happen.

I already know that Reed is going to hit my brother, and when he lands a mean punch on Ledger's face, I flinch.

I flinch even more when Ledger goes in for a payback punch.

Suddenly the crowd that had calmed down grows heated once again and somehow everyone is on everyone. There are shouts and curses and thumps and grunts.

And in the middle of it all are Ledger and Reed.

They're grappling, beating each other up. There's so much malice between them. So much pent-up aggression, years of trying to best each other, to come out on top, to bring each other down.

Years of hatred that are just pouring out on their last day of practice together.

Suddenly I realize that it doesn't matter what I tell them, my brothers, or what I tell *him* even. They're never ever going to get along.

Not if they can help it.

Chapter 8

He's sitting on the hood of his car, facing away from me, staring at something in the near darkness.

He doesn't have his hoodie on – it's May now so he shouldn't feel all that cold, but still – and through the thin material of his light-colored t-shirt, I can see the slabs of his muscled back shifting with each breath he takes.

I knew he'd be here.

At this spot, in the woods.

Located at the edge of town, where his party was that night. This is also where we usually end up when he takes me out on rides.

He looks so still, so deep in his thoughts, that I feel like I'm intruding. That I feel like I should leave him alone.

But I can't.

He hasn't said it but I know he needs me.

I know he needs *someone* by his side.

So here I am.

As it turns out, it's too late to leave anyway. Because I already have his attention.

He already knows that I'm here and he turns abruptly, his eyes zeroing in on me.

I suck in a breath then.

The moment I get to see his face.

All bruised and battered, covered with cuts. So much so that he's using his half-bunched up hoodie to put pressure on his jaw.

Back at the field, when their fight continued to escalate and a crowd was gathering, teachers were called in. They made us all leave while Conrad and the group of coaches tried to break up the fight. In the chaos of it all, I couldn't see him. I couldn't see Ledger either.

I'm pretty sure he looks the same.

My heart squeezes painfully as I study his bruises in the rapidly vanishing evening light.

Stupid soccer.

I *hate* soccer.

My thoughts break when he moves.

He takes a huge sip from the bottle that I didn't know he was holding — a liquor bottle, I presume; the liquid inside it looks as transparent as water though — and slams it down on the hood.

Throwing his hoodie aside, he springs up on his feet. "What the fuck are you doing here?"

I hug the backpack to my chest. "I came to –"

He doesn't let me speak. "Shouldn't you be at rehearsal?"

"Rehearsal is done. I –"

He fires off another question before I can finish, his eyes searching something beyond my shoulders. "How in the hell did you get here?"

"I, uh, got a ride from a friend."

His gaze comes back to me, all belligerent. "What friend?"

"From dance. Her brother was picking her up and she said that she could drop me here. It was on her way back."

His gaze grows even unfriendlier. "Her *brother.*"

"Yeah. You know him. He's a senior too. Jonathan Andrews."

This piece of information makes Reed's jaw so tight that I have to bite my lip at the force.

"Andrews gave you a ride."

"Yes. I've talked to him some and he seems nice. He's in the drama club and –"

"Fuck drama club. And fuck Jonathan Andrews." His nostrils flare. "You're going to stay away from him."

"What?"

"Stay *away*. From him," he growls angrily.

"Why?"

"Because he's got a fucking hard-on for you. That's why."

Is that why he agreed so easily?

To not only give me a ride but also to keep it a secret at school. Sophie, his sister, isn't going to be so accommodating, I know. But I'll deal with that later.

My only aim was to get to Reed.

I blink. "I didn't... He didn't... He was just trying to help me."

Reed shifts on his feet as if getting ready to do battle. "Yeah, I don't think so. What he was *trying* to do was lay down the groundwork so he could make a play for you later. So you stay away from him, you understand? He's a fucking asshole."

"And if I don't?"

His chest pushes out then and again I can see the carved muscles of his pecs, his ribs shifting under his t-shirt, making him look even more dangerous than usual.

I think the hoodie takes away from his danger, cloaks it in false softness.

Without it, he's all dense muscles and hard bones.

His hands are fisted, veins standing out on his wrists and the backs of his hands. "Then I'm going to fuck him up so badly that he won't be able to drive for the rest of his life."

I hug my backpack tightly and rub my arms, trying to chase away the goosebumps that arose at his threatening, possessive tone.

Trying to not lose my breaths all at once.

"You sound like my brothers," I say. "When they talk about you."

"For once, I agree with them." His glowing eyes narrow. "Although what *I'd* like to know is where in the fuck were they when you were getting into Andrews's car? How could they let this happen? What goddamn use are they if they can't keep you safe?"

My thighs clench together and I tell him in a breathless

tone, "They don't know. I texted Con and told him that I'd be staying late as usual. He thinks I'm at the auditorium practicing like I always do."

I did.

It was easy too.

He was expecting it even, after weeks and weeks of lying and telling him that I needed extra hours for practice.

I did need those hours.

But mostly it was because I wanted to spend them with him.

This guy who's glaring at me and who I knew wouldn't be showing up at my practice like he usually does.

"So, you lied to them," he concludes. "Again."

I nod. "I wanted to come see you."

And in this moment, I realize that even though I hate lying to my brothers and keeping secrets from them, I'll still do it. I'll still lie for him now and forever.

I'll lie and hide. I'll seek and run and stop.

I'll go wherever he is.

"You've become quite the liar, huh? For me."

"I –"

"I think you should go," he commands in a low, determined voice.

His words make me move.

But I don't do what he tells me to do.

I don't leave.

I walk toward him, bridging the distance between us.

"Did you fucking hear what I just said to you?" he asks,

agitated, watching me walk toward him.

I don't answer. I just keep walking, my backpack in hand, my eyes on his gorgeous face. Gorgeous and familiar and so achingly dear to me.

"Go home," he growls, and I keep ignoring him.

And when I finally, *finally* reach him, his face dips and his words become thick. "Get the fuck away from me, Fae."

Does he know that even when he's being all growly and stubborn and an idiot like he is being right now, he still calls me Fae?

His fairy.

And if he does that, calls me by the name he's given me, how can I ever leave?

How can I ever stop my heart from flip-flopping in my chest when I crane my neck to look up at him, at his tall form?

I shake my head. "No."

"What part of *you should go now* don't you understand? I'm –"

"I brought first aid. For your injuries." I speak over him.

"I don't need your fucking first aid."

I knew he'd say that.

So I say something else that I wanted to say. "I'm sorry."

"What?"

"For what Ledger said." I take a step closer to him, to his heat, to his violently breathing chest. "He provoked you and he shouldn't have done that. You were leaving."

He stares down at me for a moment. "Yeah well, he wasn't lying, was he?"

I raise my hand to touch his jaw where he was pressing his now discarded hoodie. But he grabs my wrist to stop me. "And I'm sorry about your dad. I don't know the why or the how or any of that stuff. But Tempest shared a little bit of it with me and –"

"Tempest should keep her mouth shut," he says with clenched teeth and his thumb mashing into my pulse.

Even so, I'm not deterred. "I-I'm here though."

"You're here for what?"

"If you ever want to talk about it."

Reed goes silent for a second as if he can't believe I said that. As if it hasn't occurred to him that *anybody* would say that. "You want me to talk about it."

"Yes." I throw him a reassuring nod. "Talking helps."

Again, he goes silent for a few seconds before he replies, "Yeah, no. Talking isn't what I had in mind. So, you should really call yourself a cab and leave."

He lets go of my wrist then, ready to dismiss me.

But he doesn't know that with nothing stopping me, I have free rein.

I have free rein to get even closer to him, free rein to put my hand on his body.

His chest.

Smooth and muscled and hard under his cotton t-shirt. Radiating heat.

As soon as I touch him though, he stops breathing. His chest ceases all motion and he lowers his eyes to look at my hand on his body.

"What is it then?" I whisper and he looks up, his wolf eyes flashing. "What's on your mind?"

The anger in him, the agitation, is palpable and when he resumes breathing, he becomes even scarier somehow.

It's like touching a wild animal, petting his hard, lethal body.

But I'm not afraid.

Because strangely I think I can tame him.

Strangely I think I'm the girl to tame this wild mustang.

"Are you sure you want me to answer that?" he asks.

His challenge only makes me caress his chest gently, tenderly, and he clenches his teeth. "Yes. Tell me."

"I'm warning you, Fae, you need to leave now."

His muscles buzz under my fingers.

As if his cold, black heart is trying to bust free from the cage of his ribs but doesn't know how yet.

"Why?"

He leans down over me, his chest pushing back against my hand. "Because my head is all fucked up right now. And this here is my second bottle of vodka. So I'm not exactly *thinking*."

In retaliation, I push him back with my hand and close that last inch between us.

So far my backpack was acting like a wall between us but I let it go now. It slips from between our bodies and crashes on the ground with a thud.

Neither of us even spares it a glance though, no.

I'm too busy finally meeting his tall, hard body with mine and he's too busy being shocked that our bodies are touching.

This isn't the first time that we've touched like this.

Of course not.

He helps me with my routine. He lifts me, assists me in my leaps and turns. He knows what my body feels like. I know what his body feels like too, all hard and smooth.

Powerful.

Like he could push mountains away to make space for his tall self and rip the earth open with his bare hands if he wanted to.

I know all that and yet I've never felt his body like this.

Just because I want to. Just because I *can*.

And neither has he.

For all his bad reputation and villainous intentions, he has not once tried anything with me. He helps me and that's it.

He's always been controlled.

Restrained.

Respectful even.

I wonder if I tell my brothers about this, about Reed's careful nature, what their reactions would be.

"I don't want you to think," I say, my neck craned up.

His stomach contracts with a large breath that he exhales as he stares down at me. "You do realize you're in the middle of nowhere, don't you?"

"Yes."

"Miles away from civilization."

"I know."

"So if you scream for help, no one is going to hear you. Not even your four older, fucking *useless* brothers whose one job was to protect you but they can't even do that right, can they?"

His rough tone makes my heart race faster. "I won't scream."

Another breath whooshes out of him. "You will. If I want you to." His eyes grow all dark just like the sky around us. "If I *make* you. And I can make you do a lot of things. In these woods, I'm the god, Fae, and my word is the only word. So if I tell you to get the fuck away from me and out of these woods, you need to do that."

I don't listen to him.

Of course I don't.

He should know by now. Just because he tells me to do something, I'm not going to do it.

Not if I don't want to.

I'm not the good girl Callie for him.

I'm his Fae and so I put my other hand on his chest too, as if to show how bad I can be, how eager.

"I'll do it," I whisper. "Whatever you want me to. I've been p-practicing."

That throws him off, my excitement, eagerness. The little tidbit of information that I let slip. I can't say that I did it accidentally. Or that I had no intention of doing it.

I had every intention.

I've had this intention for days now but I didn't know how to bring it up.

I didn't know if I *should* bring it up or not.

Given the fact that I shouldn't have been practicing at all what I've been practicing for days now.

"What?" he bites out.

If I tell him then there's no going back. Then there's no two ways about what I feel for him.

He'll know.

Reed Roman Jackson, the Wild Mustang, the soccer god, the heartbreaker of Bardstown High will know that my good girl, not-so-freshman, just turned sixteen-year-old heart beats for him; my birthday was last week and he bought me cupcakes and new knitting needles and so much yarn.

Before I can make up my mind either way, my lips seal my fate as I blurt out, "You told me the other day, in the storage closet that... that you're not so easy to take care of..."

Despite my determination in telling him, my courage falters when I actually say the words.

And I have to lower my eyes.

I have to fist his t-shirt and bite my lip as a flurry of butterflies swoops around in my stomach.

"What about it?"

His gravelly voice makes me clench my stomach. "You said that if I took care of you, I'd have bruised knees, so I..."

God, why can't I just say it?

I should be able to say it.

I started this, didn't I?

"You what?" he asks in a strangled whisper.

Finally I look up and all my fear and shyness just melt away.

He appears as he does when he watches me dance. All on edge and intense and excited. "So I get down on my knees. At night."

"On your knees."

"Yes." My knees tingle from all the abuse of the past days. "We've got hardwood floors at home. So I get down and I... I stay there."

His lips part then.

Only slightly, but I know it's because he's started to breathe heavily. His entire body is moving with it.

"For how long?" he asks gruffly.

"A long time. Until I..." I press my knees into his legs. "Until they start to feel all numb. And sore."

They do start to feel sore, after being like that for what feels like minutes and hours and days.

They do start to feel bruised up after what feels like worshipping.

Like I am praying to God.

Only my god is a devil.

A villain with wolf eyes and vampire skin.

And I feel his villainous heart skipping a beat under my fist. "You made your knees sore. For me."

"Yes," I whisper, pressing myself into him. "But that's not all. I practice something else too."

"What?"

"You said that you could... you could take care of me twice. But then I wouldn't let you. So I practice so that I will."

"How?"

My thighs clench together. "I touch myself."

"Where?"

"I… in my… you know where."

At last, he leans his face toward me, all bruised up and swollen in places, making him look like a criminal.

A thug I should run away from. But I press myself closer to.

"Pussy," he chokes out. "You touch your pussy."

I'm doused by a flood of heat at the dirty word and I nod. "Yes."

But he won't let me go so easily.

By telling him this, I've unleashed something in him. A beast, a predator, and so all I can do is revel in the fact that he finally chooses to touch me.

He not only touches me, he crushes me to him.

With his hands on my waist, his fingers digging into my soft flesh, he bends down even more, darkening the world around us.

"Say it," he growls.

"I…"

His fingers on my body grow insistent. "Say '*I touch my pussy.*'"

My own fingers dig in his chest when I obey him. "I touch my p-pussy."

"'*And I make myself come.*'"

"And I make myself come."

"For Roman."

"For my Roman."

"How many times?"

I have to gather my breaths first before I can tell him.

"T-two, sometimes three."

His eyes shoot fire. "Three."

"Yes."

"Because you were practicing."

My ballerina feet can't stay still so I go up on my tiptoes. "Yes. I wanted to be… ready."

"Ready, yeah," he whispers as well. "Because you know that if I get anywhere near that thing, it's game over, don't you? You know that I'd lick her and suck on her and fingerfuck her like I've never fucked a pussy before."

"Y-yes."

"And I'd eat her out, bang her with my tongue until she gets all sore and hurt like your knees. You know that, don't you?"

I want to say that he shouldn't curse so much.

That he shouldn't use such dirty language.

But then I'd be lying because I want him to.

I want him to say these things, I want him to talk to me like that, like he's the filthiest guy in the world and I'm the most innocent girl who's never heard these things before, the girl that he wants to corrupt.

"Yes, I know," I tell him.

"Yeah, you know that I'd become what they call me. That if I catch even a whiff of her scent, I'll go wild. I'll become an animal and I'll snap my teeth and I'll snarl. And nothing would calm me down except her, except the sight of her, the taste of her. You know I'll become a villain for your fairy pussy."

My hands creep up his chest and my fingers cradle his bruised jaw, my thumbs rubbing his stubble. "A gorgeous villain."

He presses his fingers on my waist, almost picking me up off the ground. "So you were getting her ready. Like the good girl you are. You were warming her up for me."

I wind my arms around his neck. "Uh-huh."

"In your bedroom."

"At night," I continue.

"And what were your brothers doing?"

"Sleeping."

"Where?"

"Down the hall." Something violent passes through his features so I explain, "But it's okay. Because I'm quiet. I bite on my pillow. When I come."

His jaw moves back and forth before he somehow opens his mouth and grunts, "So they don't know."

"No."

"They don't know that every night their innocent little sister touches her innocent little pussy for me. For the guy they hate."

"I don't want them to hate you," I confess.

He ignores my words and continues, "They don't know that she gets down on her knees for him. She rubs her pussy until she drips and then she bites her pillow to keep quiet. So no one ever knows what she does when she locks her door at night. And she does it all to get herself ready for the guy they've warned her about. So he could abuse that pussy and make her like it."

"I would. I would like it," I tell him as if he doesn't already know.

He swallows then. "I know you would. Because I'd make

it good for you. I'd make it so good that you'd be addicted. You'd become a junkie and you'd beg me for a fix. I told you that, didn't I? I told you that every girl begs and you will too."

My spine arches at his tone as if he's pulling on all my strings and I nod.

"Yes. I will. I'll do anything you want me to do."

"You'll beg me to spread your legs. To use that tight little fairy hole and stick it to your brothers. You'll beg me to destroy you in your good girl bedroom while they sleep just down the hall. While I make you moan in your lacy pillow and make you betray your brothers every night. And then, ask me, what will I do?"

My breaths are all but gone right now but I somehow wheeze out, "What?"

"I'll tell them," he says with a cold, humorless, half smile. "I'll tell them how pretty their sister looked when she opened her legs for me last night. I'll fucking brag about banging their sister under their noses."

"You wouldn't." I shake my head. "I trust you."

Maybe it's the stupidest thing I've ever said, even stupider than all the things I've been saying tonight, but I do.

I do trust him.

He had all the opportunity, didn't he?

He could've told them.

He could've used me against Ledger. He could've bragged if he wanted to.

But he didn't.

He kept our secret. Day after day, night after night.

I know he's trying to scare me away but I'm not going anywhere.

He scoffs. "Yeah, that's what a stupid little girl says before she gets into the car with a stranger who takes her away and locks her up in a room for the rest of her life."

"I –"

"So you need to go home, understand?" he says, letting me go. "You need to leave me alone because as I said, I'm not thinking straight right now."

"Do it," I tell him, ignoring his command for the thousandth time. "Make me do things. Everything you said. All of them. Please."

"Fae –"

"Please. Destroy me, Roman," I beg like he told me I would, and a shudder passes through him and through me too.

I stretch myself up then, as much as I can, and put my mouth on him.

On his Adam's apple.

I lick the bulge, his rough stubble, and I would've gone on to do more if he hadn't wrapped my braid around his wrist and pulled my head back.

If he hadn't made me look at him.

I shiver at the look on his face.

I shake with fear and anticipation.

His eyes have gone all dark like the night around us and his jaw has morphed into a true V. With his angry bruises, he looks so dangerous, so gorgeous that I whisper again, "Please, Roman."

At my plea, his gaze falls down to my lips and I think I hear a growl.

I can't be sure because it's low and thick and in the next second, I don't have the mental capacity to think about it anyway.

Because his mouth is on me.

His taste, all spicy and vodka-laced, explodes on my tongue and God, it's so delicious that I want to keep tasting him.

I want to keep analyzing other nuances of his flavor and his soft, warm mouth but just then, the sky opens up.

With no warning or forecast whatsoever, it starts to rain and we break apart.

Panting, we look at each other and I don't know what he's thinking.

I don't know if he's mourning the loss of my lips as I'm mourning the loss of his.

But again, he takes away my ability to think when he picks me up.

He lifts me off the ground and because we've done this move a thousand times before during my dance practice, I don't even hesitate to wrap my legs around his slim waist. And as soon as I do that, he puts his big hand on the back of my head and makes me huddle into his chest.

He makes me seek shelter from the rain in his big body.

And all I can do is take it and hug him tightly.

My Roman.

My gorgeous, *gorgeous* villain.

As he begins to move, I mumble, "My bag."

I wouldn't usually care about it, my backpack.

But it has something inside it. For him – not the first aid kit – and I don't want it to get wet.

Smoothly, while still carrying me in his arms, Reed bends down to pick up my bag. When he has it, I thank him and kiss the pulsing vein on the side of his neck. I hear him inhale sharply as he walks me to the back door of his Mustang.

He opens it and carefully deposits me inside the car, away from the rain, before getting in himself. He throws my backpack on the floor and I don't even wait for him to shut the door properly before I crawl over and straddle him.

It's such a bold move but I don't care.

I don't really care about anything tonight except being close to him, taking care of him.

Taking all his pain from the fight and his loneliness away.

My hands are on his shoulders, fisting his damp t-shirt, and his find their way back to my waist, clutching onto my wet dress. I stare at the water droplets that sluice down his dark, rain-slick hair to his beautiful face. They stream down his cheeks and the side of his neck, disappearing into the V of his t-shirt.

And God, I was right.

He's got muscles for days.

I can see them through his t-shirt, the ridges of his ribs and the hills of his chest and the cut planes of his stomach, and I squirm on his lap.

Wait a second. I'm on his lap.

How did I not notice this before?

My spread thighs, even though covered by my wet dress, rub against his damp jeans and oh my God, it's glorious, the rough fabric and my smooth skin. And so I squirm again but before I can do it one more time, he stops me.

He *physically* stops me by putting pressure on my waist and pinning me in one spot, commanding, "Hold on to your dress."

I frown. "What?"

He glances down at the hem of my dress. "Your dress. Hold on to it."

I pull at his t-shirt. "Why?"

"Just do it. Now," he says with clenched teeth, his body pulsing with his words.

I immediately let go of his t-shirt and grab the hem of my dress. He doesn't like how I've done it though, so he lets go of my waist and positions my hands.

He carefully puts my hand —*both* hands — in between my legs and makes me fist the fabric. And he makes me do it so tightly that my knuckles jut out with the force.

When he's done, he looks up. "Don't let me push it up your thighs."

My heart is banging against my chest. "Why not?"

He licks his lips, his hand flexing over mine. "Because I want to."

"But I —"

"Because I want to push your dress up and look at your panties. Because I know you're creaming them right now and I want to see. I want to look at that wet spot and picture you creaming every night for me, up in your bedroom. And if I do that, if I imagine you, then I'm going to lose whatever sanity I have left. You got that? So you're going to protect her."

"Roman –"

He lets go of my hands and buries his fingers in my wet hair.

He presses his forehead over mine as he says in a guttural voice, "No, listen to me, you're going to protect her. From *me*. You're going to hold onto your dress and you're going to guard your pussy. You're not going to let me push your dress up no matter what I do, what I say. You're not going to let me see her. Tell me you understand."

"But –"

"Tell me you understand, Fae."

It's the Fae that does it.

It's the way he says it like a plea.

Like he's the one who's begging now.

He's the one who's good and I'm the one who's bad and tormenting him. And I never *ever* want to do that. I've pushed him enough tonight, so I look into his animal eyes that look almost anguished. "If I say yes, will you kiss me then?"

His jaw clenches and he tugs on my hair. "Fuck yes."

I smile slightly and fist my dress even more tightly. "Okay. I'll hold on to my dress. I won't let you push it up. I won't let you see her. No matter what you say."

A relieved sigh escapes him then. As big a sigh as the wind around us.

And then he kisses me as he promised.

Chapter 9

Something bad is going to happen. On the field, I mean.

I don't know how I know it but I do.

It's a feeling that's been plaguing me ever since last night and somehow has been exacerbated since the championship game started.

So I finally figured out how to attend the game and my own show.

I got to the auditorium way earlier than they asked us to and got ready for my dance before I ran all the way across the school – because my auditorium and his soccer field are on opposite sides of campus from each other – to attend the game with Tempest.

But anyway, here I am, decked out in an ice blue tutu and a white leotard and full-on make-up to look like a fairy, watching the game that's about to be done in like, ten minutes.

Our team only needs one more goal in order to win and

things are looking good. Oh, and if Reed makes this goal, then he'll not only win the championship but also their contest.

Once and for all.

He's in the lead right now and he needs this last goal to seal his victory over my brother.

But I feel like something bad is going to happen.

If I'm being honest though, there's no reason for me to be feeling like this.

No reason at all. Everything is fine actually.

Everything is more than fine.

Because he kissed me. Last night.

He kissed me for a long, *long* time.

For a little while there I thought he'd never stop.

I thought *I'd* never stop.

Because when his mouth was on me, drugging me with his warm, wet kisses, I realized that I'd wanted this for so long. I'd wanted this every time he looked at me and every time he said something dirty and made me blush. I'd wanted this every time he brought me cupcakes and gave me a ride in his Mustang.

So yeah, for a little while there, he became my entire world.

Reed Roman Jackson and his mouth and his Mustang with foggy windows.

His Mustang in which I came.

Well, I came on his lap. Twice.

Because he wasn't happy with just once and wouldn't stop kissing me or rocking me in his lap. And like the ballerina I am, I danced and writhed as much as he wanted me to.

After two though, I told him to stop, as he predicted days and days ago, and for which I'd practiced like a good girl.

But instead of reminding me that all my practice failed, his gray eyes simply turned all soft and liquid and he kissed me on my sweaty forehead, making me burrow into his chest.

God.

I never ever imagined that he could be so... tender and sweet and just everything.

Anyway, after that I gave him his present.

The one I had in my backpack.

It's something that I've been working on for the past several weeks.

A sweater.

"Because you're always cold," I told him, because he always is.

That's why he wears his hoodies practically all the time.

"And because white's your favorite color, and look." I pointed to the black intarsia that I'd done on the front. "It's a mustang. An actual mustang, not the car. Oh and it was my very first intarsia project. It came out nice, right?"

I'd seen the pattern in a knitting book months ago – before I really knew him – and it'd reminded me of him.

So when I decided to knit for him, I went and dug the magazine up and well, I stabbed myself in the fingers with the needles a million times before I got the design right.

Reed didn't say anything. Not for a long time as he stared down at the sweater I made for him and I had to ask, "You don't like it?" I started pulling it away from his grip, which was surprisingly tight. "It's okay. Don't worry about it. I'm gonna make you another one and –"

"I like it," he said in a hoarse whisper, speaking over me.

And then he pulled me to him and pressed his mouth on my forehead.

He didn't kiss me there again though, no.

He just… breathed with an open mouth for a few moments like he couldn't get enough air and I let him.

That was all.

That was all that happened last night.

We kissed, he made me come, I gave him his present and then he drove me back to school just in time for Con to pick me up from the parking lot.

I haven't seen him since.

Which is understandable given the fact that his big game is currently underway, and I've been busy with my own practice for the show.

Maybe that's why I'm feeling uneasy.

Because of the championship game.

Because I know how important it is to him and to Ledger. Oh, and it's also the last game of their high school career.

Not to mention their last game together.

It should make me happy that they won't butt heads anymore — they're both going to different colleges on soccer scholarships — and this contest, no matter who wins, will finally be over.

But strangely I'm uneasy.

Ledger's in possession of the ball and he's running across

the field with it. Just when he reaches a point where he can take a shot and score the goal, the winning goal no less, Reed barges in.

He swipes the ball from Ledger and there ensues a struggle between the two star players of Bardstown High.

They both grapple for the ball, trying to score the goal, somehow dodging the players from the opposite team as well.

Not that I had any doubts that they wouldn't be able to.

Together, the Mustang and the Thorn can defeat every single team in the state and they have. They're that talented.

I'm not afraid that they'll lose the ball.

I'm afraid about something else.

Something that happens right in front of my eyes.

While struggling to get the ball, they're both pushing at each other.

Until Ledger stops.

He comes to a dead halt because Reed has said something.

I see his lips move – the lips that I kissed last night in the rain and then in his Mustang, the lips that have made me smile and blush over the past months – and I see Ledger freezing over.

To the point where Reed finally steals the ball from my brother and scores the goal.

Sealing both the championship and his victory over my brother.

As the whole stadium erupts in cheers and laughter and happiness, I sit in my spot tense and shocked, afraid.

So afraid.

My eyes are glued to two of the most important people

in my life.

He is that, isn't he?

Somehow Reed Roman Jackson, *my* Roman, has become one of the most important people in my life and I don't want to keep him a secret.

This is another thing that I've been feeling ever since last night.

Along with this premonition, I've been wanting to tell my brothers about him. Make them understand that he's not as bad as they all think he is.

But like yesterday at practice when they fought, Reed is in no mood to be good.

Even though he's gotten the thing that he wanted, the title of reigning champion, his mood is so black and so bitter that even I can feel it from here.

Even I can feel his fury.

And the only thing that matches Reed's fury and his agitated breaths as he glares at my brother while the Mustang camp of the team pats him on the back, is Ledger.

He matches Reed's black mood.

In fact, he's surpassed it.

And it's nothing new, see.

Reed has always been the one to provoke my brother and my brother has always been the one to give in to it.

So this scene shouldn't be too alarming, but it is for so many reasons, and when Ledger closes the distance between them, I can't sit still.

And neither can Tempest, who's also been glued to her

spot through all the happiness and enthusiasm around us. To-gether, we manage to grapple through the thick, happy crowd and bound down the stairs to get to the front.

So we can see what's happening.

So we can see if our brothers are okay.

God, please let them be okay.

Please.

I'm chanting it in my head all through the journey that should've only been a few seconds but takes an age due to the excited and exiting crowd.

When we do reach our destination, I exhale a relieved breath.

But it only lasts for a few seconds.

Because the moment we get to the front and have a clear view of the field, somehow, *someway*, he sees me.

His eyes fall on me through the incoming crowd, through all the chaos, and I don't know what I see in the depths of them.

I don't understand the intense emotion reflected in them and it scares me even more.

It scares me that as he runs his eyes over my body it feels like the last time. Like he'll never see me again after this.

Like this is goodbye.

Before I can do anything about it, jump the fence and run to him or something like that, my brother turns to look at me too.

And as soon as *his* eyes fall on me, that dark brown that I've known for as long as I've lived and that has never ever looked at me with anything less than affection even when we've fought,

I take a step back.

My knees tremble.

There's such hatred in them.

Such thick and pervasive betrayal that I don't know how to breathe.

I don't know how to live on to the next moment, and then he turns back around and before I can even blink, he punches Reed in the face.

That punch is all it takes.

It makes the already wild crowd go wilder and crazier and a riot breaks out.

On the field, in the bleachers and like yesterday at practice, everyone is on everyone. Only this is much, much bigger in scale and much more horrifying.

So much so that I think I'll get crushed under it.

Under the mad crowd and the insanity.

Somehow I don't though because Tempest grabs my hand and pulls me away. She drags me through the crowd, dodging people and keeping a firm grip on my hand.

I'm thankful for it.

Because if it wasn't for her, I'd be on the ground. My legs wouldn't hold me under the weight of my brother's gaze.

Under the weight of *his* gaze too.

The guy I'm in love with.

I'm in love with him, aren't I?

I love Reed and *God*, I don't know what just happened and I…

Finally, I can breathe because we're out at the entrance

now. It's not as if the crowd has thinned out but the space is more open and air is easier to get.

I see security flooding onto the field, where the fight is still going on.

I can't see Ledger or Reed and I turn to Tempest, with a pounding heart. "I need to go find them."

"Wait, what about your show?" she asks, still holding on to my arm.

Oh.

My show.

That's about to start in less than ten minutes and they must be wondering where I went.

"I don't… I need to find out what happened. I need to… I need to go."

I let go of her hand and enter the field.

I start running toward the huddle, which is slowly getting controlled by security and teachers and coaches.

But I don't make it too far because I see someone I recognize.

Conrad.

My oldest brother.

He's somehow emerged from the huddle and is now marching toward me.

In fact, he's almost here and he looks furious. I'm used to him looking all intimidating and large but when he wears a suit with a tie — which he only does for championship games — he appears even scarier.

But I can't let that deter me.

I need to know what happened. What Reed said and why Ledger looked at me like he hated me.

When Con reaches me, I immediately break out with my questions. "What happened? I…" I glance to the crowd. "Is Ledger okay? Is… What happened, Con?"

My oldest brother grinds his jaw as he looks down at me, and even though his navy blue eyes don't hold the same hatred, my heart shrivels even more.

"Con, what happened? Please tell me. I –"

My brother grabs my arm then and starts dragging me away from the commotion.

I look back but still can't see Ledger or Reed or get any indication if they're going to be okay.

"What are you doing?" I ask my brother as I turn back around. "What… Con."

He comes to a halt in a relatively quiet and isolated spot along the bleachers, his face all tight and bunched. "You've been lying to us. You've been lying to Ledger."

"What?"

He stares at me for a beat before shaking his head. "All this time, we trusted you. I trusted you. I gave you everything you asked for. Every freedom, every comfort. And you've been lying. All those late practice hours." He shakes his head again. "I thought you were smarter than this, Callie. I thought my sister was…"

His jaw tics as he plows his hand through his hair and I watch him, watch my brother's face, drenched in disappointment.

I watch his face tighten with anger and betrayal.

Betrayal that I caused. That he somehow found out about.

God, he found out about it.

He somehow *knows*.

And with trembling lips, I have to ask, "How did you..."

"The boy you were lying for all this time, he was bragging about you on the field."

I'll brag about how pretty their sister looked the next day...

That's why Ledger looked so betrayed, didn't he?

That's why there was so much hatred in his eyes when he looked at me.

No, no, no.

He wouldn't do that. He promised me.

He promised.

He wouldn't break his promise like this.

He *wouldn't*.

I somehow pull myself together and say, "There has to be a reason. There has to be an explanation."

"Explanation."

I flinch at Con's angry voice but still, I grab his arm and plead with him, "Con, he's not like that. He's not. I know you hate him. I know Ledger hates him too but he's not all bad. He's not. You don't know him like I do. You don't..." I gather my scattered breaths again. "I was going to tell you, I promise. I was. I just... I'm sorry that I lied. I'm so sorry. But Con, there has to be an explanation for this. If I could just —"

"Enough," he snaps, making me shut my mouth and let

go of his arm. Then he pulls in a deep breath, as if to calm himself. "We'll talk about this later, you understand? Go back to your show right now. You've got a show, remember?"

"I don't care about the show, Con. I need to see if Ledger's okay and I need to talk –"

"All you need to do is go back to the show. You need to go dance and we'll talk about this later, got it?" he orders. "Straight to your show, Callie. You're done wasting your time on him."

Chapter 10

I watch him from across the space.

He's sitting on an overcrowded couch with a bunch of his friends. There are girls in the mix, of course. But he's not paying attention to any of them.

In fact, all his attention is on his bottle.

The same one as yesterday. The liquor that looks like water, vodka.

Even though he's focusing on the alcohol, I'm still jealous of all the girls around him. I'm still jealous that they're trying to get his attention like they always do.

I want his attention.

I just don't know how to get it.

I'm too afraid to walk up to him.

I'm too afraid to ask him.

I'm too afraid...

Come on, Callie. Do it.

That's what you came here for, right?

Right.

That's why I abandoned my show and came to this place.

This place outside of my town where this strange party is happening and Reed is in attendance.

After Con told me to go back to the show, Tempest found me again. She dragged me away from the crowd and took me to a quiet place, away from the stadium.

Away from all the people, from all the violence.

Even she knew I couldn't dance like this.

She stayed with me as I cried and shook.

As my whole body was wracked with waves and waves of chills.

She stayed with me as I ran through a thousand different scenarios in my head. As I went over what I saw and what Con told me and what I know.

What I know in my heart about Reed.

About my Roman.

I'm not sure how long I stayed like that, huddled into myself with Tempest rubbing my back and my arms.

All I know is that when I could gather my strength, I asked her to find him.

I asked her to take me to him.

And despite vehemently disagreeing with it at first and saying that I needed to go home and take care of myself, she brought me here.

She said that she saw it on social media. Someone had tagged Reed on Instagram, saying that he was at a party outside of Bardstown.

So that's where I am, at a party, watching the guy I'm in love with chugging down vodka, surrounded by a drunk crowd.

I try to make myself move.

I try to make myself call out his name, wave at him, do something to catch his attention. But I'm just frozen in my spot, too scared to move.

A second later though, I don't have to.

Because as always, he senses me.

He looks up from the bottle and his eyes land on me instantly and they start to glow.

His wolf eyes.

They sparkle as he stands up from the couch and starts walking toward me, leaving everything behind.

The crowd parts for him as he approaches me, his gaze growing heavier and more intense with every step he takes.

The moment he reaches me and stops, I realize that he's wearing all black.

I don't know why that's important.

I don't know why I'm thinking about his black t-shirt paired with dark jeans. I don't know why I find his black leather jacket intimidating and dangerous, but I do.

I'm thinking about how all this darkness makes his vampire skin come alive.

How his bruises, old and new, come alive as well.

How he's too beautiful for words.

Too otherworldly. Too gorgeous.

He looks down at me with a strange kind of tenderness

as he takes in my costume, my make-up that's ruined now, and my blonde hair twisted into a bun, which again is ruined, strands hanging around my face in tatters.

But the way his eyes melt at the sight of me makes me think that I'm the most beautiful girl he's ever seen.

It makes me think that *I'm* too beautiful for words. Too otherworldly. Too gorgeous.

"Fae," he whispers roughly, drunkenly. "You're here."

"Roman –"

"You look like a fairy," he says over me, bringing his hand up and tracing a finger down my cheek.

My mouth parts at his touch and the world disappears.

And I think, *you look like a villain.*

That's what he looks like, isn't it?

Dressed in black and dark bruises, the guy I'm in love with looks like a villain.

"Are you drunk?" I ask instead.

He looks down at the bottle in his hand. "A little."

I swallow painfully. Thickly.

Fearfully.

"I won," he says then, his busted lips stretching up in a smile.

A smile that looks so misplaced, so boyish and adorable on his sharp, villainous face.

"You –"

"I fucking won the game, Fae. I won. I'm the goddamn champion. Did you see?"

My eyes sting as I nod.

"You did, huh? I was pretty badass out there." Chuckling, he takes a sip of his vodka. "More than your fucking brother."

"What –"

"Hey, what about your show?" he asks, speaking over me again. "Fuck, did I miss it?"

"I don't care about the show. I –"

"If after all that practice, I missed your first-class, fantastic show, then I'm an asshole. I'm a motherfucking asshole. You should be mad at me. Here." He waves his free hand. "Hit me. Slap me in the face, Fae. Slap me in the fucking face –"

"No, Roman, listen to me." I speak over him, putting an end to his drunken rambling. "What happened?"

He appears perplexed. "When?"

I shake my head. "On the field. What happened?" I swallow again. "God, look at you. You're all banged up. What happened, Roman?"

He chuckles. "You should see the other guy."

"What did you say to him?"

"What did I say to whom?"

I fist my hands for a second, trying to keep my wits about me. Then, "Roman, please, okay? Can you focus for a second? Just... please. What did you say to my brother? What did you say to Ledger? Why did he... Why did he punch you? Why did you guys fight?"

I'm not sure if he's getting the gravity of the situation because his reaction is pretty casual.

His reaction is to squint his eyes slightly and shrug. "Ah, that. The fight."

"What happened, Roman?"

He takes a gulp of his vodka, swallowing loudly. "Yeah, I might have mentioned something."

My heart thuds. "W-what?"

He shrugs again. "I might've said something about me giving you a ride in my Mustang. About you loving it and fogging up my windows." A frown. "Not in those words though. I was dirtier than that but you know what I mean."

"Y-you what?"

Reed sighs then. "Look, I just wanted to piss him off, all right. He was gonna score. I had to do something. It was the championship game. My last chance to win."

"Your last chance to win."

"Yeah, I just wanted to win." He bends down slightly. "But if it makes you feel any better, I only won by two goals. Your brother was a worthy opponent. You should tell him that tonight. Tell him I said that. Tell him Reed said that he's good. A real pain in my ass with how good he is. But you know, the best man won. Tell him to not cry too much in his pillow."

There's a pain in my chest. A massive, gigantic pain, but I power through.

I power through because this isn't real, right?

This isn't him.

This isn't how he behaves.

He's never this drunk. He's never this... cruel.

He's had plenty of opportunities to *be* cruel.

He's had plenty of opportunities to be a player, a heart-breaker, to be all those things that they call him, but he's never taken them.

No, this isn't him.

He's never broken a promise to me and I refuse to believe that he did now.

Even though I saw it with my own eyes. Even though I saw it in my brothers' eyes, both Conrad's and Ledger's.

"What are you doing?" I burst out, desperately. "Why are you acting this way?

He thinks about it for a second. "I'm not acting."

"You promised," I remind him. "You made that pact with Ledger, remember? The pact that you were so crazy about. You promised you wouldn't tell. You promised you wouldn't use me against Ledger. You promised me that the first time I danced for you. You had tons of opportunities to do that but you never did and –"

"Right. I lied."

"What?"

He drinks from his bottle again. "I lied. I made it all up."

"You lied."

"Yeah. I kinda do that." He shrugs again. "One of my many bad habits but I try to love myself for who I am. I think self-acceptance is a very intriguing concept. It basically –"

I grab his t-shirt in my fists and snap, "Stop."

Finally, I think I've jerked him awake.

Finally, I think he's seeing me, hearing me.

So I tell him, "This isn't you. This isn't how you behave. I know it. I know. People are wrong about you. They think you're selfish and you're a jerk and you're bad. But you're not. You love your sister. You take care of her. You take care of *me*. You're not cruel. You're not. You protected me, Roman. Last night. I thought about it."

I nod and fist his t-shirt even tighter. "I did. I thought about why you didn't… have sex with me. It didn't occur to me until after you dropped me off at the school parking lot. You were protecting me, weren't you? You wanted to protect my innocence. That's why you told me to hold on to my dress. That's why you didn't even *ask* me to take care of you. You didn't and –"

Reed grabs onto my fists on his t-shirt and the muscles in his stomach contract as he growls, "This is starting to really piss me off now. I was having a good day, all right? I won. Yeah, I also got beaten up for it by your wonderful brother, who packs a really mean punch by the way. But it's fine. I don't care. I'm the champion. I've been waiting for this day ever since your brother stole the title last season. So yeah, I was having a brilliant fucking day and I would really like to get back to it. So I'm going to make this really easy for you.

"These past few weeks have been good. Fun. I mean, I still don't like twirling but I can see why dudes do it. And I'm not sure if I'm going to be walking into that cupcake store again. It's too pink for me. But I have to say that it's been interesting. Given the fact that the only reason it all started was because you're the Thorn Princess. But you're really fucking ruining it right now."

"What did you just s-say?"

"Look, it was a clear-cut way to mess with him. It's not as if I was thinking about it. It's not as if I was plotting ways to seduce my rival's little sister. But then you walked into my party looking all sweet and innocent. I tried to stay away, trust me. I even made that stupid fucking pact. But then you were so interested in me. I mean, why wouldn't you be? Every girl is, but I would have had to be stupid not to take it. I would have had to be too stupid not to take you. Especially when it was too easy to reel you in. Too easy to take you for a ride, make you do things. You practically stood on the edge of a cliff for me. All I had to do was give you a push. All I had to do was make you fall."

All he had to do was give me a push.

He's right.

I stood on the edge for him. My arms wide open, wearing a white dress.

And all he had to do was nudge me a little.

All he had to do was make me fall.

"You did all this so you could mess with Ledger," I whisper as numbness spreads through my veins.

His jaw clenches. "I did all this for soccer."

"So you could beat him."

"So I could beat him."

I repeat his words from a long time ago. "Because winning is everything."

"Yeah." His eyes flick back and forth between mine. "Besides, I showed you a good time, didn't I? So no hard feelings."

"No hard feelings."

"In fact, you should be thanking me."

I dig my fists into his torso. "I should be *thanking* you."

"Yes. For the fact that I made sure there was minimal damage."

"What minimal damage?"

Reed lowers his voice then, staring at me with flashing eyes. "I didn't fuck you, did I? I could've. But I didn't, and trust me, that was hard. It's not every day a guy gets a lap dance from a horny ballerina. I've had my fair share of cheerleaders and I know how bendy they can be. I know how bendy *you* could be. I've seen you dance.

"And some guys don't like virgins. They say they're too much work. You can't fuck them how you want to. But I'm not one of those guys. I like them. I like training them. I like breaking them in. I like when they bite their lip and make those hurting noises. I like when they push you away like it's too much for them. But you rub them in the right place and they cling to you like you're their entire world. I like that. I liked how you clung to me and how when you came, you looked like you couldn't believe it. You looked like nothing had ever been that good. And I could've rocked your world last night. Even more than I did. But I didn't. I let you go. So yeah, minimal damage."

"Why? Why did you let me go?"

"Consider this my good deed. Of the month." He thinks about it. "Year. I let you escape my evil clutches unscathed. Your brothers should thank me. It was torturous." He looks me up and down. "It still is. And if you don't want me to pick you up and carry you to my Mustang and drive you back to those woods and give you a *real* reason to spin and bend over like the pretty blonde ballerina you are, you should really let me go, Fae."

I do.

I let him go.

I step back from him.

Not because of what he said he'd do if I didn't.

But because of Fae.

Because he called me by the name he gave me.

A fake name.

A name that I held dear to my heart like a fool.

I clung to it at night. I put it under my pillow like a wish.

A name that made me feel like a real fairy.

His fairy.

"You're an asshole," I breathe out and almost cringe.

He said all these things to me and this is what I say to him?

This is *all* that I say to him?

This is the extent of my wrath?

"Now you know," he drawls.

"I can't believe I..." I trail off because I don't know what to say.

I don't know what to think. What to feel...

I wrap my arms around my waist and bite my lip before trying again. "So stupid..." I shake my head, unseeing. "I can't believe I've been so stupid. I... God, I've been so foolish. I thought you... I fell in l –"

"You're not going to say the L word, are you?" he says, cutting me off.

I draw back, as if he has struck me.

"Well, you were," he murmurs and all I can do is stare at him silently.

All I can do is stare at the guy who's standing in front of

me in dark clothes, not one ounce of softness on him, staring back at me with emotionless wolf eyes as he says, "Let me tell you something about guys like me. Guys like me, we like to play. We like to break hearts. Just because we can. Just because it's fun. You don't *fall* for guys like me. You don't pin your dreams and hopes on guys like me. You don't lie for them. You don't sneak around for them. You don't knit them sweaters. You called me a villain, remember? That's what I am. I like breaking hearts. I like breaking lovestruck dreams. I like feeding on the innocent love of innocent girls like you. What I don't like is for that girl to stand in front of me and cry about it. I thought I told you that the only thing I love is my Mustang. I thought you understood. I thought you were smarter than that. I thought your brothers taught you everything."

Smarter than that.

That's what Con said to me, didn't he?

He said that I was smarter.

He said that he trusted me.

And I lied to him.

I lied to all of them. To him, to Ledger.

Especially to Ledger.

The brother I have betrayed the most. I don't even know how he is. I haven't even seen him since the fight.

Because I came here.

Because I came running here to see the guy who lied to me.

Who lied and used me.

For soccer.

Who played with me and broke my heart because he wanted to win at a game.

I shake my head again, my vision getting blurred. "Yeah, I thought that too. I thought my brothers taught me everything. But apparently, they didn't. Apparently, I'm just a stupid girl who fell for a villain."

His features are tight now, stark and gorgeous and heartbreaking. "Well, consider this your first lesson in love and growing up."

Yeah, my first lesson in heartbreak.

"See you around, Fae."

With that he leaves.

As abruptly as he came into my life.

He walks back to that couch where the whole world is waiting for him with open arms. While mine is crumbling around me.

While my world is plagued with earthquakes and landslides, his simply blooms and sparkles, teeming with a new life, a new adventure.

He's going to New York this fall, isn't he?

Foolishly, I thought that we'd still keep in touch. That we'd find a way to be together. I even thought about spending the last month of school… being with him now that the championship game was over. Hanging out with him in the hallways, in the courtyard. Listening to music in his Mustang.

Yeah, I thought that.

In the deepest recess of my mind, I did think about life after the soccer rivalry comes to an end and after he leaves Bardstown High.

But as I found out tonight, I'm stupid.

And in love. With a villain.

With a guy who likes to break hearts.

***

I don't remember walking out of that party.

I don't remember finding Tempest out in the driveway either.

All I remember is that I'm here.

I'm outside, under the starry night and my best friend has a hold of my arm. She's trying to get my attention. She's asking me something, I know that.

But I'm too distracted.

I'm too focused on something that I saw as soon as I came outside.

In fact, it's the first thing I remember seeing: a flash of white.

A bright, sparkly white.

Brighter than the moon even.

A white Mustang.

His white Mustang.

The only thing he loves.

That's what he just said.

He said that the only thing he loves is his Mustang, and then all the numbness, all the fog that had surrounded me ever since he told me the truth, his truth, vanishes.

I turn to Tempest. "I-I need the keys to his car."

"What? Why?"

"I just… I need…"

Tempest grabs my shoulders and makes me look at her. "What happened, Callie? What did he do? What'd he say to you?"

I look at her, into her gray eyes, so much like her brother's. "I love him."

Sympathy overcomes her features. "I know."

"He used me."

"What?"

I have to wait for this pain in my chest to pass before I can speak. "H-he said he used me. Against Ledger. He did it all to mess with him. So he could win at soccer."

Her eyes are wide. "Oh God."

"I don't… I don't know how to stop this."

"Stop what?"

"This pain," I whisper. "I don't know how to make it stop hurting."

She hugs me then. "Oh, Callie. I'm so sorry. I'm…" She moves away from me. "Listen, Callie, my brother, I love him, okay? I love him to pieces, but he has a major self-destructive streak. He can be… toxic and –"

"Will you bring his keys to me?" I ask, cutting her off.

"Keys to his Mustang?"

"The thing he loves the most."

She studies me for a few seconds before nodding with determination. "Yeah. I will. Just wait here."

And I do.

And she does too.

She does bring me the keys after a few seconds and I don't ask her how she did it. How she swiped her brother's keys.

All I do is get inside his car and despite my many protests, Tempest gets inside too. All I do is start his car and drive away.

I'm sixteen now so I can get my driver's license.

In fact, Con was going to take me for my test next weekend and he's been teaching me for the past few months. Ledger has been teaching me too.

Him too.

He's the one who taught me to drive stick. He's the one who taught me that in his Mustang.

So this isn't the first time I'm driving this car.

Although this is the first time I'm driving it to this place.

I've been to this place before. With my brothers and a couple of times with my friends.

Never with him though.

I regret that.

It would've been poetic. Me driving to a place in his stolen car that we used to visit together.

But it's not.

It's tragic and catastrophic and awful.

Just like our Shakespearean names.

It didn't help, did it?

Changing them, calling each other by made up names. Rivalry and hatred still fucking won and it's so awful that I'm cursing and I don't even mind.

It's so awful that when I get there, to my destination, the

lake, I stop the car.

I turn to Tempest. "I'm going to do something awful."

"I know," she says.

I flex my fingers on the wheel. "Aren't you going to stop me? He's your brother."

Tempest throws me a sad smile. "He's my brother, yes, and that's why I know that he must've done something really horrible for you to do this. I know what my brother is capable of, Callie. I know he broke your heart. I know he didn't just break your heart, he smashed it. Didn't he?"

A tear streaks down my cheek as I nod.

"Well, then I was right. You wouldn't do this otherwise."

That's all the encouragement I need.

I turn back and look at the lake, all shimmering and silvery under the moon, surrounded by trees. A slope leads down to it, a perfect slope for what I have in mind.

I start the car and pull at the gear. I put it in neutral and say to Tempest, "Get out now."

She does and I'm right behind her.

And then, standing on the forest floor, my ballet flats crunching the leaves and tears streaming down my face, I watch the love of his life sliding toward the lake at a steady pace.

Before it hits the water.

Before the water slowly engulfs it, swallows it down, eats it up like he ate up my heart.

Just when it looks like I'll never see it again, something goes off inside of me. Another earthquake. Another explosion, and I start to run toward the lake.

I start to dash toward it but Tempest stops me.

She grabs my arm and pulls me back. "Callie, no. Let it go."

"No, I can't... I..."

"Hey, it's okay. It's fine. Let it go."

"I have to... I have to save his car. I have to..."

"Callie, you can't go in there, okay? You can't."

"But I have to save it." It's going down and down, the bright white disappearing into the darkness. "I have to... He loves it and I... I can't hurt him like this. I can't hurt him..."

"Hey, hey, Callie. Look at me." She turns me around and shakes me, makes me look at her. "It's just a car, okay? It's only a car."

"But he loves it," I tell her, tears streaming down my face.

"He'll get over it."

"I have to save it," I whisper.

"You don't."

"I have to save the thing he loves."

"No, not right now, okay?" She hugs me again. "Right now, you just need to save yourself."

And then I can't stop crying.

I can't stop sobbing as I cling to my friend.

I cling to her like she'll save me like I want to save his car.

But the truth is that no one can save me.

I'm already dying.

I've already fallen in love with a villain.

ABOUT

THE AUTHOR

Writer of bad romances. Aspiring Lana Del Rey of the Book World.

Saffron A. Kent is a USA Today Bestselling Author of Contemporary and New Adult romance.

She has an MFA in Creative Writing and she lives in New York City with her nerdy and supportive husband, along with a million and one books.

She also blogs. Her musings related to life, writing, books and everything in between can be found in her JOURNAL on her website.
www.thesaffronkent.com